BOB
VS
THE SELFIE ZOMBIES

ANDY JONES

Illustrated by Robin Boyden

Piccadilly
PRESS

First published in Great Britain in 2023 by
PICCADILLY PRESS
4th Floor, Victoria House, Bloomsbury Square
London WC1B 4DA
Owned by Bonnier Books
Sveavägen 56, Stockholm, Sweden
www.piccadillypress.co.uk

A CIP catalogue record for this book is available from the British Library.

ISBN: 978-1-80078-348-5
Also available as an ebook

1

Typeset by Emily Bornoff
Printed and bound in Great Britain by Clays Ltd, Elcograf S.p.A.

Piccadilly Press is an imprint of Bonnier Books UK
www.bonnierbooks.co.uk

To Me

As this is a book about time travel, perhaps I am
allowed to dedicate it to someone from the past.
Perhaps I will dedicate it to eleven-year-old me.
Andrew, it must seem incredible to think you grow
up to become an author. But trust me, kiddo, you
can do it. Just pay attention in English class, OK?
Oh, and grow your hair long while you still can.

'I never think of the future – it comes soon enough.'

– Albert Einstein, mathematical genius.

'Time flies like an arrow. Fruit flies like a banana.'

– Author unknown. But still a genius.

THE PRESENT NOWISH

A CONFUSING PLACE.
A FISH-FINGER CHOO-CHOO.
TIME GOES FAST.
A CRACKLE BENEATH THE TABLE.

Mum wasn't the best cook in the world. I mean, if she had been, she'd have worked as Head Dinner Lady at a ten-star restaurant instead of in a garage as a mechanic. But she was a good cook. Even if her hands were usually covered in engine grease. She baked pies, cooked casseroles, made her own pizzas. She cooked Spanish food, Sri-Lankan, Mexican. Mum said the kitchen was her 'happy place', and I honestly believe you could taste that in her cooking.

Dad – if I had to guess – would say the kitchen is his 'very confusing place'. And you can taste that in his cooking. Which is unfortunate now that he has to prepare all our meals.

He's fine with the simple stuff – sausages, burgers, chips and so on. It's when he tries to actually cook that things get . . . interesting. Chicken and pineapple pie, baked bean and tuna curry, stilton and egg pizza. It's not the worst food in the world. It's just . . . weird, I suppose is the kindest way of putting it. Even my dog Zem (who's favourite things to eat include shoes, sticks and sheep poo) turns his old wet nose up at Dad's cooking.

Luckily, it's fish fingers, chips and peas tonight, and the opportunities for Dad to mess it up are relatively small. Although, as he places my supper on the table, I see he has created another food sculpture.

I started big school this year, but Dad still likes to arrange my food into the shapes of faces, animals, tanks, volcanoes, rockets and whatnot. As if I was still nine or ten years old, not eleven and a bunch of months. Honestly!

He's looking at me now, waiting for me to say something about his latest creation.

'What is it?' I don't mean to sound sulky, but that's the way it comes out.

'It's a choo-choo,' says Dad.

'You mean a train.'

'*Choo-choo*,' says Dad, pulling an invisible steam whistle. He grins.

I don't.

'What's up?' says Dad. 'You used to love choo-choo trains.'

'I also used to like shoving crayons up my nose. I'm not a baby any more, Dad.'

'No one's saying you're a baby. It's just . . . you know, I thought it was fun.'

And, looking at it again, I suppose the train is kind of cool. Four fish-finger carriages lined up on a circle of French-fry train tracks.

'What are these?' I say, pointing at a row of peas.

'Passengers,' says Dad. 'They're pea-ple. Get it?'

'I get it,' I say, smiling. 'It's awful, but I get it.'

Dad shrugs. 'I'm a dad. It's my duty to make awful jokes.'

'Sorry for being grumpy.'

'We all get grumpy,' Dad says. 'Grumpy is allowed. But just . . . don't be in such a hurry to grow up, OK?'

'OK,' I say, loading my fork with a slice of fish-finger train carriage and a few pea-ple.

'It'll come soon enough. Time goes fast,' Dad says, clicking his fingers. 'Trust me.'

I scoop up a forkful of supper, but a single pea drops to the table and rolls onto the floor.

'Escap-pea!' says Dad.

'Good one,' I tell him.

Zem, sensing food, climbs out of his basket and hoovers up the little green escap-pea. Beneath the table, something makes a muffled, crackly sound.

My first thought is that he's farted.

This would be very bad news indeed. Zem is a big, old dog and he has been known to clear a room with a single – often silent – dog-guff. He has been known, in fact, to clear an entire village hall. In a competition for the world's most toxic dog-parps, Zem would be World Champion. Although why anyone would arrange a competition like that, I have no idea.

The crackling sound happens again. Dad and I swap worried looks. And then – just as we're about to run from the kitchen – I remember that I have my walkie-talkie between my legs. It crackles a third time, immediately followed by the voice of my best friend.

'Bob. Bob, are you there? Over?'

Dad gives me a stern-ish look. 'What have I told you about walkie-talkies at the table, Bob?'

'Well, strictly speaking, it's below the table,' I say.

'Hmmmmm,' says Dad.

'Bob?' says the walkie-talkie. 'You there, Bob? Over.'

Dad smiles and nods at me: Answer it.

'I'm here,' I say into the walkie-talkie. 'Over.'

'Ready for rehearsal?' says Malcolm. 'Over.'

'Just got to finish my supper. Over.'

'Whatchahavin? Over.'

'Fish fingers. Over.'

'Did he arrange them? Over.'

I glance at Dad. His expression gives nothing away.

'Train,' I say to Malcolm. 'Chips for tracks.'

'Cool,' says my best friend.

Dad clears his throat, glances at my supper, mouths the word: Supper. Mouths the word: Over.

'Got to go,' I say to Malcolm. 'See you in the garage in ten minutes. Over.'

'See you there. Over and out.'

I put the walkie-talkie down and stab my fork into a few chip train tracks.

'Make sure to chew that properly,' Dad says. 'You know, choo-choo it properly.'

And when he laughs, it makes me laugh too.

THE TENTACLES OF TIME.
THE SCHNITZEL.
A TALENT SHOW.
PUKING ON A TRAMPOLINE.

Our band is called the Tentacles of Time. There are eight reasons for this.

1) Our band is a rock band, and rock bands need names that sound a bit tough and a lot cool.

2) Our real names do not sound tough. They do not sound cool. I present you with:

Malcolm Schnitzel: Guitar and shouting

Robert Trebor: Drums and wailing

Trebor and Schnitzel — we sound like a pair of bakers or grave-diggers or drain-unblockers. Instead of a wicked cool rock band. So, no real names.

3) Tentacles, though, sounds exactly the right amount of tough and cool.

4) And it rhymes perfectly with the science word for goolies.

5) Also, I like stuff about time.

6) On account of me being a time traveller.

7) Not that Schnitzel believes me, but he likes the name anyway.

8) I don't really have any more reasons, but what with tentacles normally coming in eights, it felt weird having a list of seven.

We almost didn't enter Griffin's Got Talent, because of school talent competitions not being particularly cool. But first prize is £50's worth of vouchers for the local shopping centre, where we could spend the prize money on getting band T-shirts printed.

Malcolm, as well as being a not-too-terrible

guitarist, is an amazing artist and he's designed a logo for the band. It's an octopus playing a guitar, grabbing a microphone, smashing up a clock and generally thrashing about. For £50 we can get two T-shirts printed with the rock octopus on it and still have some money left over for sweets.

Tonight is our final rehearsal for the big show.

It is – clearly – a very important rehearsal.

We need to be focused.

We need to be professional.

We need to practise until our fingers are raw.

But not so raw that we can't actually play tomorrow.

Just sort of a bit tender.

Except, 'practise until our fingers are tender' doesn't sound very rock 'n' roll.

But you get the point. It's important.

I tap my stick against the rim of the drum to count us in for our final – did I mention it's important? – rehearsal.

'A one, a two, a one two three f—'

'Say cheese!!!'

I pause with my drumstick in mid-air and turn towards Malcolm. What he should be doing is playing his electric guitar. He should be making the ground shake with powerful rock music. He should be rehearsing.

This is not what Malcolm is doing.

Malcolm, with his school tie knotted around his forehead, is holding his phone in front of his face and grinning like a chimpanzee in a banana factory.

'What are you doing, Malcolm?'

'Band selfie,' he says. 'For history, for when we're famous.'

'Malcolm, we are never going to get famous if you keep wasting precious rehearsal time taking selfies.'

'Band selfies,' Malcolm corrects, as if this makes even the slightest difference.

He's still holding his camera at arm's length, still

grinning like a monkey, still – apparently – determined to take his band selfie.

'Smiiiiiile,' says Malcolm.

I'm not sure if what I do with my mouth really counts as a smile, but I at least show my teeth.

'Perfect,' says Malcolm.

'Fine,' I say. 'Now perhaps we can get on with rehearsing.'

'You bet,' says the Schnitzel. 'Let's do it.'

I tap my sticks on the rim of my drum. 'A one, a two, a one two three f—'

'Boys!' says a voice.

And even before I turn my head, I know exactly who it is.

Allow me to introduce Gloria Dizamale. Gloria Dizamale (also known as Gloria Dismal. Also also known as the Dismal One) has been my next-door neighbour for five years. She has been a source of constant embarrassment and annoyance ever since my mother invited 'Dismal' to my sixth birthday party. Where she ate too much cheesy pasta then barfed all over my birthday present – a brand new trampoline.

Puking while bouncing on a trampoline is bad enough, but my new neighbour wasn't just bouncing, she was rotating, so that her cheesy vomit sprayed in a full circle, coating the nets, the floor and everyone else on the trampoline. You'd think most people, after throwing up their party lunch all over a trampoline and several young children, might stop bouncing. Not Gloria Dismal. She just kept on jumping and twisting and puking like it was some kind of performance at the world's worst and grossest circus.

The party was ruined – children screaming, mothers screaming, fathers laughing so hard they had tears in their eyes. It was like something from a scary movie.

Five years later, I can still hear those people screaming. And on a hot day, I can still smell cheese sick on my trampoline.

I never invited Gloria Dismal to a birthday party again, but what with her being my next-door neighbour she just turns up anyway. Not that anyone will go on the trampoline with her. And not that Dismal cares.

I read that vampires can only come into your house if you invite them. I don't know why anyone would do that – invite a bloodsucking monster into their house – but it's reassuring to know you have the option not to. Gloria Dismal is not like that.

She just barges in whenever she feels like.

Like this evening, slap bang in the middle of our final rehearsal.

It serves me right for not closing the garage door.

Our garage is at the bottom of a long and steep driveway, and Dismal crouches low on her skateboard as she hurtles towards us at terrifying speed. Sunlight flashes off her mirrored helmet as she swerves around Schnitzel's bike, jumps a garden gnome and skids to a stop, inches from my drum kit.

'Boys!' she says, flipping her deck and catching it in one hand. 'Looks like I'm just in time.'

'Do you mind?' I say. 'We're kind of busy.'

Written down, that may sound reasonably polite (or politely reasonable, for that matter), but the way I said it – the grumpiness in my voice, the frown on my face – should make it clear that what I am really saying is, 'Oi, Dismal, get the heck out of here.'

But this is Gloria Dismal we're talking about.

'Course, I don't mind,' she says, removing her helmet and freeing her hair, which springs up and out in one hundred thousand thick black curls.

'We're trying to rehearse,' I say to Gloria. 'Big competition tomorrow.'

Dismal flops down in Dad's wheelbarrow, her legs dangling over the edge as if it were some kind of velvet sofa. 'I know,' she says. 'And I'm here to help.'

'Help? We don't need help.'

Gloria looks first at me then at Malcolm. 'Hate to break it to you boys, but I've heard you rehearse, and yes, you do. There's a lot of tough competition. Lot of talented acts.'

'What,' I say, laughing, 'like Maria Mamooli and her hamsters?'

'Hamster juggling is a real talent,' says Malcolm.

'I'm more worried about Eno,' says Gloria.

Eno Fezzinuff – he's Year 7 like us, but is already the smartest kid in Griffin High School. Or at least that's what Eno likes to tell everyone.

'Apparently he's invented something,' says Gloria.

'Inventing's not a talent,' I say. 'Anyone can invent. Banging drums is a talent. And the Tentacles of Time do not need any help, thank you very much.'

'You need a better song,' says Dismal.

'How dare you!' I say. 'How absolutely dare you!'

'It doesn't even make sense,' says Gloria.

THE TENTACLES OF TIME

Lyrics: Trebor and Schnitzel

Hey yeah, we're the Tentacles of Time.
And we've got eight arms like an Octopus
Except we don't mean it literally
Because we've only got the two of us.

Tentacles, Tentacles, the Tentacles of Time
Yeah yeah yeah we're the Tentacles
The Tentacles of Time.

[CONTINUED]

WE DARE TO BE DIFFERENT.
A TAMBOURINE.
ENO FEZZINUFF.
AND THEN IT HAPPENS . . .

'It makes perfect sense,' I say. 'The only thing here that doesn't make any sense is you.'

'What about the bit with you having eight arms even though there's only two of you?'

'That's creativity!' I snap.

'And it's a bit short,' Dismal continues. 'It only has one verse.'

'Verse schmerse. We're rockers. We're rule-breakers, we dare to be different.'

'In which case . . .' says Gloria, beaming as if she's just lured me into a trap, 'I have just the thing.'

As always, she is carrying a massive shoulder bag, which she now roots through as if looking for lost treasure. The bag is almost as big as Gloria, and it crosses my mind to pop her inside it, carry it back to her house and dump her on her own doorstep. But like I said, the bag is only almost as big as the Dismal One. Even with folding, I couldn't squeeze all of her in.

Dismal is busy pulling things from her giant bag. Scattered around her feet are a ball of wool and a pair of knitting needles, a half-knitted scarf, some leaves, four slightly brown bananas, a pair of joke glasses with spring-loaded eyes, a notebook and a pencil with a big fluffy thing on the end.

'Dismal,' I say, 'this is a band practice, not a jumble sale.'

'Ta da!' says Dismal, pulling a tambourine from her

bag and giving it a little shake.

'A tambourine?'

Dismal grins, nods, and gives the tambourine another rattle. 'Good, isn't it?'

'Gloria, we are a rock band. A hard rock band. And you cannot – under any circumstances – be a hard rocker with a tambourine.'

'Just because no one has,' she says, 'doesn't mean no one can.'

Gloria Dismal stares at me. Her eyes are large and wide and unblinking as she fixes me with her gaze. It's very unsettling.

'I . . . I don't want to,' I say, and my voice sounds weak under the full force of Gloria's powerful stare.

'Can't hurt,' says Schnitzel, the absolute fink.

Gloria hops out of the wheelbarrow in one – I have to admit it – rather impressive movement. 'Give it a shake,' she says. 'You might like it.'

'Will not.'

'Might.'

'Get back,' I say. 'Get that thing away from me.'

Gloria begins walking towards me like some sort of tambourine-wielding zombie.

'Schnitzel!' I say, my voice tight with panic. 'Call her off. Stop her!'

Dismal laughs.

Schnitzel laughs.

And then someone else laughs. It's the sort of laugh an evil villain would have if he was an eleven-year-old boy with a slightly breaky voice. As if my afternoon wasn't going badly enough, now I have to deal with this.

'Eno,' I say, with a sigh.

And there he is – Eno Fezzinuff, sitting astride his bicycle at the top of my drive and looking – as he always does – immensely pleased with himself.

I really should learn to close the garage door.

'I wouldn't waste my time practising if I were you,' says Eno. 'Everybody knows I'm going to win Griffin's

Got Talent. The rest of you are there to witness my greatness and nothing more. History, if it remembers you at all, will remember you as' – he holds up the finger and thumb of one hand in the shape of a capital letter L – 'losers.'

'Witness this,' says Gloria, holding up her tambourine and pretending to Frisbee it at Eno's head.

Eno flinches. 'Careful! You could have somebody's eye out with that thing.'

'Shoo,' says Gloria, rattling her tambourine at him. 'Before I really do throw it.'

'Fine,' says Eno. 'I'm going. But only because I'm bored with you.' And with that he sets off pedalling down the road and out of sight.

And then he pedals right back into sight.

He has attached a series of small lights to the spokes of his bike, and as the wheels turn, the lights spell out the word: losers.

Eno laughs his squeaky villainous laugh, and this time, when he vanishes from sight, he stays vanished.

Even so, the whole series of events has left me feeling all stressed and jittery.

'Don't worry about Eno,' says Gloria. 'He's just jealous of us.'

'Us?' I say. 'Who said anything about us?'

'I did,' says Gloria. 'Just now.'

And again she rattles her tambourine.

But now her voice and the instrument sound faint and far away.

My hands are tingling, my head has gone fuzzy, there is a feeling of wet pressure all over my body and I realise what's about to happen about one and a half seconds before it happens.

And then it happens.

What Time Travelling Feels Like

It comes on slowly, a tingle in the middle of me, in my bones, in my blood, in my brain. Like hundreds of tiny ants crawling underneath my skin. That's the time-tingles, and if you're thinking it sounds absolutely hideous, you'd be absolutely right.

Next I get the drags. A feeling like being pulled in eight different directions. Like having a giant octopus wrap its tentacles around my arms, legs, body and head and then doing the octopus equivalent of the splits.

Then, just when it feels as if I'm about to be turned into a wet quivering pile of spare parts . . . Pop! I've travelled in time. Maybe a few minutes, maybe several years. But always forward. Always to the future.

It's confusing, frightening and a real pain in the bum. Particularly if you're in the middle of something important, like . . . like your last band practice on the day before the school talent show.

THE FUTURE
2043

3

A DROPPED CAKE.
A BIG BLUE-HAIRED BRUTE.
A FADED SCAR.
AN URN.

Someone is screaming.

At first I think it's me, and if it was, well who could blame me?

But it's not me; it's a fully grown man. And he's a big one.

He's as wide as a fridge-freezer and just as tall; taller if you account for his spiky blue hair. His thick arms are covered in tattoos, he wears a ring through the side of his nose, and has the kind of beard that would make a Viking jealous.

He'd look terrifying if he wasn't so clearly terrified himself.

At the man's feet is a great pile of steaming yellow mess that looks a lot like a dropped cake. Banana cake, judging by the smell.

The great brute backs away from me until he bumps into the fridge (nearly knocking it over in the process), his eyes never leaving mine, as if I might bite, as if I might explode, as if I've just materialised in the middle of the kitchen.

'He just materialised in the middle of the kitchen,' says the man. 'It's . . . it's . . . impossible.'

'Stay calm,' says a steady voice behind me. 'Take a breath, Malcolm. Everything is going to be OK.'

Malcolm? This big blue-haired brute is Malcolm?

I turn around to face the owner of the calm, steady voice.

'Hello, Bob,' he says.

The man squats down so his face is level with mine.

He tilts his head backwards, and even with his stubble, I can see the long white scar under his chin. The scar from when I slid the wrong way down the fireman's pole in the playground last summer.

'You're me,' I say.

The man nods. 'And you used to be me.'

'Scar's faded.'

'Well,' says the man, 'it's been twenty years.'

'So this is . . . ?'

'2043,' says the man. 'Welcome to the future, Bob.'

Before today, the furthest I'd travelled was just over four years into the future, to a point where my teenage self was trying to grow a moustache. This trip is huge by comparison, and the future version of myself is a fully grown man with stubble and long hair showing around the sides of a backwards-facing baseball cap. He wears yellow high-top trainers criss-crossed with purple laces, skinny black jeans, and a leather jacket over what looks to be an Iron Man T-shirt.

'You grew up,' I say.

'Trying not to,' he laughs.

I glance around the kitchen, only now paying attention to the way it's been decorated. Each of the four walls is painted a different colour – pink, green, blue, yellow. Pictures of famous rock bands – the Rolling Stones, The Who, AC/DC – hang on the walls. There is a pinball machine in one corner, an old-fashioned jukebox for playing records in another.

For some reason, I have never thought about how I would decorate my kitchen when I become a grown-up rock star, but now that I'm standing in it, I have to say, I have done an excellent job.

And then I notice . . .

The table and chairs are very familiar. So are the tiles on the floor, the cookbooks on the shelves, the magnets on the fridge, the apron being worn by the big man cowering against the fridge . . . This is my kitchen. This is my house.

'You still live at home?' I say to Future Me.

He nods.

'You still live with Dad? I still live with my dad?'

Future Me laughs. 'Give me some credit. This is my place now. Dad's moved on. Gone somewhere smaller.' As he says this, Future Me casts his eyes towards the large kitchen window.

I follow his eyes, take in the superhero figures standing on the windowsill, the cobweb in the corner, the potted plant that looks like it needs watering. I take in all of this, and then I see the urn. And I know it's an urn because I've seen one before. It looks like a fancy jar, black and polished, with a gold lid. The surface is speckled with a scattering of silver stars. It looks like the kind of thing Gandalf might use to store special wizard stuff – gems maybe, a genie perhaps, or a heap of magic dust. But urns like this – they hold a different kind of dust. They hold the ashes of the dead.

'How did he die?' I say, my bottom lip beginning to

tremble and making the words all wobbly.

'Who?' says Future Me, looking through the window.

'Dad,' I say, jabbing my finger firmly at the urn.

'Hey,' says Future Me in a soothing voice, 'Dad's not dead. Dad's fine. Well, he's gone a bit bonkers – but he's fine. He moved into a small cottage by the seaside.'

The feeling of relief is so powerful it makes my knees weak. I couldn't handle losing another parent. Especially as I was just having supper with Dad about thirty minutes ago.

I point at the urn. 'So who's in there?'

'That's Zem,' says Future Me with a sad smile. 'You know about Zem, right?'

In my present, Zem is twelve years old, which is ancient for a dog. And – thanks to me being a time traveller – I know that he has another three years before he dies peacefully in his sleep, aged around a hundred and five in dog years. I'm absolutely dreading it happening in my own time, but it's not, I suppose, what you'd call tragic. Tragic is when someone dies too young. When someone is taken from you too soon. Trust me, I know.

'Yes,' I say. 'Fifteen-year-old us told me.'

'How is Zem?' says Future Me.

'Still doing toxic guffs,' I say.

Future Me laughs. 'It's good to know he's still . . . you know, out there somewhere.'

I nod at my dog's urn. 'Didn't fifteen-year-old me – fifteen-year-old us – didn't he keep his ashes in a shoebox?'

'Fifteen-year-old me did all kinds of strange things. As you will soon discover. But about ten years ago, twenty-year-old me decided our friend deserved something a bit less . . .'

'Cardboardy?'

'Exactly,' says Future Me. 'Less cardboardy.'

'Ahem,' says the enormous man backed up against the fridge. 'Hate to interrupt your little catch-up, but would someone like to explain WHAT THE HECK IS GOING ON HERE?'

We sit at the kitchen table. Me, Future Me and Malcolm. In the centre of the table is a baking tin full of freshly baked and recently dropped banana bread. The three of us look at each other silently, each waiting for someone to speak, but none of us knowing exactly what to say or where to start.

Malcolm fiddles with the ring through his nose, looks like he's about to say something, then shakes his head and gives his nose ring another tug.

My tummy gurgles.

It's a side-effect of time travel. I haven't eaten since suppertime in the year 2023, which, when you think about it, was around twenty years ago. But although this cake smells fantastic, it looks terrible. A smashed pile of steaming yellow goo covered with bits of muck and fluff from the kitchen floor.

My tummy gurgles again. It sounds like bathwater swirling down a plughole.

'Excuse me.'

Malcolm narrows his eyes at me. His lips move silently as if he wants to say something but can't find the right words. He stares at me the way you might stare at an optical illusion, as if his eyes and his brain are in disagreement about what exactly they are dealing with here.

He blinks. 'He's . . . real?'

'Real as you and me,' says Future Me.

'Maybe twice as real,' I say.

'How?' says the enormous man who used to be my best friend, who – it would seem – is still my best friend.

'Here we go again,' say me and Future Me at exactly the same time.

'Again?' says Schnitzel.

'Again,' say both of me.

Some Stuff About Time Travel

My first jolt into the future happened less than a year ago.

One day after my eleventh birthday.

One day after the worst day of my life.

I was lying in the bath, feeling gigantically sorry for myself, thinking about what had happened, about what I'd said, and wishing I could go back in time – just one day – so I could make it right.

That's when it happened.

I was wishing I could go back, when – somehow – I went approximately ten minutes forward. I don't know about you, but I take my baths in the nude. Bearing this in mind, it was lucky that I only travelled from one time to another, and not – like I sometimes do – from one place to another. Imagine travelling ten minutes forward in time, stark bottom naked, and ending up, for example, in the supermarket, at school or the top of a double-decker bus. Even the idea of it makes me blush.

Luckily for me, that first time I time travelled I landed in the same place I started out. Which is to say, the bath. The water had cooled by this point, but that wasn't the only thing that gave me goosebumps. The other thing was this: there was now another me in the bath. Ten minutes older, hair washed, and sleeping – a dangerous thing to do in a bathtub.

I did the only sensible thing to do in the situation. I screamed. Ten-minutes-in-the-future Me's eyes snapped wide open, he sat upright, he screamed.

Then I jolted ten minutes backwards; the water was warm again, I was alone, and I was very confused. Had I really been asleep? Was I still asleep? Was this whole thing a dream? I hadn't slept much at all the night before, so it was possible.

I pinched myself.

It hurt.

So I was awake. Or maybe I was simply dreaming

that I'd pinched myself and dreaming that it hurt. My dreams can be very realistic. Which, I suppose, makes the whole pinching-yourself-to-see-if-you're dreaming thing kind of pointless.

I certainly felt awake. My heart was beating hard, my mind was buzzing with ideas and possibilities and there was absolutely no danger of me nodding off in the tub. Which was probably a good thing.

I pinched myself again, just to make sure. It still hurt.

I sat in the bathwater thinking all of this until my fingers wrinkled and the water began to cool. And then time caught up with itself and the me from ten minutes ago suddenly materialised in my bathtub.

We screamed.

Again.

And then past me vanished – presumably returning to the past so he could think about what had happened and give himself a couple of good pinches.

About three weeks later, I travelled again.

Not in the bath, thankfully, but in my bedroom, where fifteen-year-old me was making a mess of his history homework. (Question: Who was the Duke of Wellington's major rival? Future Me's answer: The Earl of Flip-flop.)

That time, me and fifteen-year-old me managed to talk instead of just screaming. It might only have been the second time for me, but fifteen-year-old me had time travelled dozens of times, and he sat me down and explained a few things. These are those things:

1) Time travel is bouncy. Like trampolining into the future. No matter how far I travel, something time-gravity, maybe – always brings me back to present. The first time I travelled it was a single bounce – ten minutes forward and ten back. But the time after that, when I travelled four years, I bounced in and out of the future four times.

Stick around and you'll see what I'm talking about.

2) There tends to be a reason for my travel. Some problem Future Me is having – from small stuff like messing up his homework, to slightly more serious stuff like nearly drowning in the bathtub.

3) What else fifteen-year-old Future Me told me was that he has seen nineteen future versions of ourselves, and sixteen future versions of Malcolm. And every time we see a new Malcolm, he screams as if it was the first time.

4) Because for Malcolm, it always is the first time. Every time I go back to my present, everything resets. The old future is erased and a brand new one is written on the clean white pages of time. (Not my words, by the way. This is how fifteen-year-old me explained it to eleven-year-old me, and even though he's trying to grow a moustache and smells a bit funny, I think he puts it quite well.)

5) Finally, he told me this: anything about time travel that doesn't make sense is what scientists call a 'time-travel paradox'. (A paradox, apparently, being something that is brain-meltingly complicated and confusing.) And the very fact that time-travel paradoxes exist, is proof that time travel itself exists. Otherwise, how could there be any time-travel paradoxes?

Makes perfect sense to me.

TATTOOS AND NANOBOTS.
GURGLING.
WHAT HAPPENED TO THE BANANAS?
A GIRL.

My best friend drums his fingers on the table and his tattoos ripple over his gigantic forearms.

'It's just not possible. Is it?'

'What did you just see?' says Future Me. 'With your own eyes?'

Malcolm shrugs. He sticks out his bottom lip like an enormous sulky child.

'Come on,' says Future Me. 'Tell us what you saw?'

'Saw a boy,' says Malcolm.

'Doing what?' coaxes Future Me.

'Materialising out of thin air,' says Malcolm.

'And who does that boy look like?' says Future Me.

He pouts his lip again. 'Looks like you.'

'Exactly,' says my future self. 'He looks like me. Because he is me. Because I – as I have explained – am a time traveller.'

'But it's impossible,' says Malcolm.

'Now now,' says Future Me, wagging a finger. 'We've been through this already. And unless you have a better explanation, I suggest we just accept the evidence and move on. Do you have a better explanation, Malcolm?'

Malcolm pouts. But he shakes his head while he's doing it.

'Great,' says Future Me. 'I'm glad we cleared that up.'

'Did you know he was coming?' says Schnitzel. 'Do you remember it happening from when you were him?'

Future Me shakes his head. 'You can't remember

45

what hasn't happened yet. This is the start of a brand new trip for both of us.' He ruffles my hair, which is both weird and annoying. 'I don't remember it any more than this young man does.'

'I suppose that's another of those paradoxes,' says Malcolm.

'Exactly.'

Malcolm scratches at his beard. He has a tattoo of an octopus on his arm and one of the tentacles stretches across the back of his hand. As he fidgets with his beard, it looks as if he's being attacked by a tiny but determined sea monster.

'Nice tattoo,' I say.

'Thank you. I did them myself. I'm a tattoo artist.'

'That's wicked,' I say. 'You always were good at art.'

Malcolm nods. 'Thank you. Although tattooing has as much to do with computer programming as it does with drawing these days.'

'What?'

'I'll show you,' says Malcolm, pushing a button on his watch.

There is a small hum in the air, Malcolm's hair wilts – the spikes softening and lying flat. The colour drains from his hair too, the peacock blue replaced with Malcolm's familiar dark-brown colouring. At the same time, his tattoos fade and vanish, as if being rubbed out by some invisible eraser.

'What just happened?'

'Nanobots,' says Malcolm.

'Nanowhatnots?'

'Tiny little roboty things under the skin,' says Future Me.

'They were designed for medical purposes,' says the Schnitz, 'but this is way cooler.'

I glance at my future self, looking for tattoos and piercings. 'Do you have nanobots?'

Future Me laughs. 'I'm cool enough already.'

'Debatable,' says Future Malcolm.

He chuckles for a moment and then he catches my eye, remembers he's sitting opposite a time traveller, and his laughter fades.

'So what now?' says Malcolm. 'Is he stuck here? Do we have to send him back? Wire him up to a big clock in a thunderstorm or something?'

'I do have a name, you know,' I say. 'And you're not wiring me up to anything, thank you very much.'

'Sorry,' says Malcolm. 'It's all a bit, you know . . .'

'Weird,' I say. 'I know.'

'Bob is going to be coming and going for a while,' says Future Me. 'And it's going to be confusing for all of us. But when it's over, when everything is back to something like normal, I'll do my best to explain. But for now, can you just . . . trust me?'

'That you're a time traveller?'

'Yes.'

'That you exit one reality and somehow appear in another?'

'Yup.'

'That the established rules of the known physical universe don't apply to you?'

Future Me nods. 'That pretty much sums it up.'

Schnitzel considers this silently. He looks from one of us to the other and back again. Considers a bit more, then shrugs.

I mean, what else can he do?

'Fine,' says Schnitzel. 'And you promise he's not going to kill me? That neither of you are . . . you know, evil?'

'Bob's not going to kill you,' says Future Me, crossing his heart. 'At least not on purpose. And, no, I'm not evil. I fart on the bus sometimes, but I always say excuse me under my breath.'

'That's disgusting,' says Malcolm.

'I said I'm not evil,' says Future Me. 'I never said I was perfect.'

Malcolm turns to me. 'And what about him?'

'Not evil,' I say. 'And before you ask; no, I don't fart on the bus.'

My stomach makes a loud burbling noise.

'You sure about that?'

'I haven't eaten for twenty years,' I tell him. 'Got any biscuits?'

'Sorry,' says Future Me. 'We're all out.'

'Crisps?'

He shakes his head apologetically.

'Got anything?'

'Absolutely nothing,' says Future Me. 'I've been putting off going to the shops until I really really need to.'

'Wise,' says Malcolm. 'Very wise.'

'Eat the banana bread,' says Future Me with a nod towards the tin of destroyed baking.

'It's been on the floor!'

'Not for long,' he says. 'And the floor was cleaned three days ago. It'll be fine.'

I pick the least fluff-stuck piece I can find and pop it into my mouth. And then spit it straight back out.

'Bleauurghh!!!'

'Charming,' says Future Me.

'That's disgusting,' I say, but, as I'm wiping my tongue with my sleeve, it comes out more like, 'Blats blispusping!'

Still, Future Me gets my meaning. He takes a piece, chews it slowly and swallows. 'It's fine,' he says, but his expression says he isn't convinced.

'That,' I say, 'is not fine. That is revolting. Worse than revolting – it's like a broken promise in a cake tin. I smell banana, but it tastes like . . . like a child drew a banana in yellow crayon on a piece of cardboard, shoved it in a tin and called it a cake. It's the least banana-y tasting thing I've ever tasted.'

Now Malcolm takes a piece of cake. He chews, he frowns, he spits the cake into the palm of his hand. 'He might have a point,' he says. 'I'm trying to remember what originanas taste like, but . . . I don't think they tasted like this.'

'Whoa,' I say. 'Originanas? What's originanas?'

Malcolm looks at me thoughtfully. 'He really is from the past, isn't he?'

He says 'the past' as if it's some remote village deep in the rainforest, one without electricity or indoor plumbing.

'Originanas,' says Future Me, 'is short for original bananas.'

'What are they?'

'Just bananas,' says Malcolm. 'But they're extremely rare now. By weight, they're more expensive than silver.'

'Why? What happened?'

'Selective farming,' says Future Me. 'Lack of genetic variation. Yield and durability dynamics. Commercial pressure, market forces, economic imperatives, big banana fungus, then whoops-a-daisy, where did all the bananas go?'

'You seem to know an awful lot about it.'

Future Me smiles with no small amount of pride. 'I'm a teacher.'

'You. Are. Not!'

He nods. 'Am.'

I stare at him in disbelief. 'I've spent my whole life waiting to finish school and you . . .' I level my finger at him, 'you go and get a job as a . . .' I can hardly bring myself to say the word, '. . . a teacher.'

'It's very rewarding,' says the Future Mr Trebor.

'But what about all this?' I gesture around the room, at the pinball machine, the jukebox, the superhero figures on the windowsill. 'What about all that?' I indicate his clothes; the skinny jeans, the fat trainers, the backwards-facing baseball cap.

'What about it?'

'You look ridiculous.'

'You didn't seem to mind it ten minutes ago,' says Future Me.

'Ten minutes ago I thought you were a rockstar, not a . . . teacher.'

'Well, that's just stereotyping, Bob. I'm disappointed in you.'

I feel exactly like I've been told off by a teacher.

Which I suppose I have.

Except the teacher is me.

It's very confusing.

'What do you teach?'

'History.'

'But you hate history.'

'Only the boring bits,' says Future Me.

'Don't you have to teach those bits?'

'Every job has its issues,' says Future Me. 'But at least this one is important.'

'History? How is history important? Maths, maybe. English, possibly. But history? History's just a massive waste of time.'

The future Mr Trebor laughs. 'History is the essence

of time, actually. Without history, we'd have no future. And where would we be then?'

I've never been any good at history, and now I feel like I'm on the spot in the classroom again. 'In a world with no bananas?' I try.

'Exactly,' says Mr Trebor. 'Well done, Bob.'

I point to the fluffy mush in the centre of the table. 'So what on earth is this?

'Instant cake mix with a dash of bananish powder.'

Here we go again: 'Bananish?'

'Genetically engineered banana essence,' says Malcolm. 'It's amazing what they can do these days.'

'It would be if it didn't taste like crayons,' I say.

Future Me's head slumps into his hands. 'The kid's right. This is a disaster. Even if you hadn't dropped it, it would still be a disaster. A hollow gesture. A farce, a fiasco, a failure of imagination and romance. What am I going to do, Malcolm? She's going to be here in a couple of hours and all I've got is a steaming great pile of ish!

Ish, I tell you! Complete and utter ish!'

I clear my throat. 'I'm not really sure what you're going on about. But for a moment there, it sounded like you said romance.'

'That's right,' says Future Me with a dopey grin on his face. 'Romance. We're in love, Bob.'

'You're in love,' I say. 'With a girl?'

'A woman,' says Future Me.

'But girls are . . . odd. They wear tops with animals on them. They do strange things with their hair. They paint their nails. They dance. They make that loud squealy noise. They skip. They make daisy chains. They pay attention in class. Girls eat their vegetables. Girls bake. They draw love hearts on top of the letter i. I don't understand girls.'

Future Me smiles his dippy smile. 'I know,' he says. 'Isn't it wonderful.'

'How is it wonderful?'

'It's hard to explain,' says Future Me with a look I

don't like one bit. 'But you'll know it when you feel it.'

'I will not! I refuse to feel anything at all if it's got anything to do with . . . girls.'

'A woman,' says Future Me. 'And what a woman! She is the twinkle in my eye. The spring in my step. The fizz in my lemonade. I'd climb a mountain just to be by her side. I'd swim the deepest sea, for just a glimpse of her smile. I'd –'

'Bake her a loaf of fake banana bread?' I say.

Future Me sighs heavily. 'It's hopeless,' he says. 'Hopeless.'

And now I feel bad for bursting his bubble. Even if it is a love bubble.

'What's so important about this banana bread?' I say. 'Can't you just . . . give her a biscuit?'

'Banana bread's her favourite,' says Future Me. 'I was going to hide an engagement ring inside it. I can hardly hide an engagement ring inside a biscuit, can I?'

It occurs to me that this depends on the biscuit. A digestive? No. But a Jammy Dodger, possibly. And those big domey chocolate ones with marshmallow in the middle? Definitely. But it also occurs to me that my future self just said the words 'engagement ring'.

'You're going to ask this woman to marry you?'

'That was the plan,' says Future Me.

'Who is she? Who are you inviting into our life? I demand to know!'

'All you need to know is that I love her, I'm going to propose to her, and I'm going to do it with a loaf of banana bread. Made with real bananas. I am going' – he shoves his chair back from the table, stands and thumps his fist against his chest – 'to the shops!'

It's the sort of performance you might expect of someone who has just pulled on a suit of armour, clutched his sword, mounted a horse and set off to slay a dragon. It is not at all the kind of performance you would expect from someone who has just grabbed a carrier bag so they can pop down to the shops.

Malcolm stares at my future self with something that looks like alarm. 'The shops?' he says. 'Are you sure?'

'Positive,' says Future Me. 'Stay here if you want, but I have to do this.' And again, he thumps himself on the chest.

It really is quite a carry-on, and as my future self does his strange little routine, I begin to feel unusual. My fingers and toes tingle. The skin on my head prickles. And either I'm coming down with flu, or here come the tingles.

Now Malcolm pushes back his own chair and stands.

'I'm coming,' he says. 'What kind of friend would I be if I let you go out there on your own?' He pushes a button on his watch; his hair forms into blue spikes and a swarm of colourful tattoos slither into place beneath the surface of his arms.

'OK,' says Future Me. 'Let's get kitted up.'

'Kitted up?' I say.

'Helmets, sunglasses, baseball bats,' says Malcolm. 'Standard stuff.'

'Seems a bit extreme for a trip to the supermarket?'

'Things have changed since you were a kid,' says Future Me.

'I'm still a kid,' I remind him. 'And what do you mean, things have changed?'

'The sun's quite strong,' says Malcolm.

'So it's a bit warm?'

'And the world has been overrun by zombies,' says Future Me.

Wait.

What?

Zombies.

And now I feel the pressure; the heavy, icky push and squeeze of the drags. My vision blurs, and any second now the forces of time will take hold of me and pull me back to my present and my future self's past.

'Zombies?' I say, but my voice sounds thin and distant.

Everything fades to black.

And I'm gone.

A GREAT BIG PAUSE BUTTON.
FLYING SPIDERS.
THIN WALLS.
SHAKE-A-SHAKE-A-SHAKE-A.

'Bob. Bob? Bob!'

I'm back in the garage, sitting behind my drum kit, my sticks raised ready to count us into our final rehearsal. Malcolm is standing beside me with a school tie knotted around his head and his guitar in his hand. So this must be after he's taken his band selfie.

And before Gloria Dismal crashes our practice.

'Bob,' says Malcolm. 'Are you OK?'

'Been better,' I tell him.

'You went a bit weird there.'

By weird, Malcolm doesn't mean – you just vanished into thin air and then suddenly reappeared. That's not how it works in the present. As far as I can tell, everything in the present just sort of . . . freezes. And when I return, it simply continues as normal. Like someone has pushed a great big pause button on the present.

Malcolm won't notice a thing.

Me? I feel as if I've been buried in wet sand, dug up again, turned upside down and swung around by the ankles. So can you blame me if I 'went a bit weird'?

'You were muttering something about zombies,' says Malcolm.

'Right,' I say. 'That makes sense.'

'Actually,' says the Schnitz, 'it makes no sense at all.'

'I'm fine,' I tell him. 'I can explain everything. Well, I can try. But first I need to close the garage door.'

'Why? What's going on?'

'Dismal's coming,' I say, running across to the big

swing door. 'If we're quiet, she might get bored and go away.'

Malcolm looks towards the driveway. 'I don't see anything. Don't hear anything.'

'Trust me. She's coming.'

I have to jump to reach the handle, but I get it first time and the garage door swings smoothly to the ground.

'But how do you know Glo—'

I hold a finger to my lips. 'Shh . . .'

And there it is – the familiar sound of Dismal approaching on her skateboard. I crouch down behind the door, making myself as still and silent as possible.

Now the sound of Dismal's skateboard turning into the drive.

It picks up speed.

There is a change in the sound as she swerves around Schnitzel's bike.

A moment of silence as she jumps a garden gnome.

And the sound of skidding wheels as she stops in front of the closed garage door.

Bang, bang, bang!

The garage door rattles as Dismal thumps or kicks it from the other side. 'Hello? Anyone there? Bob. Malcolm. Helloooo?'

I look at Malcolm as if to say, I told you so.

Malcolm looks at me as if to say, How did you know?

'I know you're in there,' shouts the Dismal One. 'I heard you. Heard you through the walls.'

And then she hammers on the door again: Bang, bang, bang!

Something tickles the end of my nose and I have a sudden urge to sneeze. I control myself, brush at my face and, when I look down at my hand, I see a dirty great spider. Heavy, hairy and legs as thick as lollipop sticks.

I shake my hand, trying to get rid of the revolting creature, but it's holding on tight and those hairy legs are strong. I flap my hand again, and fling my arm forward as if throwing a cricket ball. The spider flies through the air, heading straight for the Schnitz who – big mistake – opens his mouth in a silent scream.

The spider lands in Malcolm's mouth.

Malcolm's mouth snaps shut.

He screams with his eyes. They bulge in horror and he leaps up and down, as if his trousers were on fire. He runs around in small circles, flapping his arms like a pigeon that's forgotten how to fly. His face turns red and he shakes his head from side to side as if . . . well, as if he has a dirty great spider in his mouth.

Somehow, though, Malcolm manages to do all of this – the dancing, flapping, bulging and generally freaking out – without making a single sound.

Gloria bangs on the door.

'Hello hello helloooo?!'

Malcolm stops dancing. He freezes. He opens his mouth.

I don't know if spiders can look shocked, but something about the way this one crawls out of Malcolm's mouth suggests that it is. It pops its head past Malcolm's lips, as if checking for danger, then leaps to the floor and makes a run for a dark corner of the garage, presumably very much relieved not to have ended up as some eleven-year-old boy's supper.

Malcolm stands still for a moment, closes his mouth, and a massive shudder passes through his body.

'Anyone?' says Gloria, on the other side of the door.

My heart is beating so hard that I hold a hand to my chest to stop the sound echoing off the garage walls.

'I guess there's no one here,' says Dismal.

And then I hear the sound of her skateboard rolling up the driveway and away. I count to five inside my head then let out a long breath of relief.

'That,' says Malcolm, 'was weird!'

'I know. The spider was literally inside your mouth. How did you not scream?'

'I'm not talking about the spider,' says Malcolm. 'Although it was – by a mile – the most disgusting thing that has ever happened to me in my entire life. I'm talking about how you knew Gloria was coming.'

'Ah, that.'

'Yes,' says Malcolm. 'That.'

Malcolm is my best friend, so, of course, I have told him about my time-travelling adventures. But Malcolm is also – despite some of the things he does – a reasonably sensible eleven-year-old boy. So, of course, when I say – for example – 'Hey, Malcolm, I just travelled four years into the future and helped my teenage self with his history homework,' Malcolm does not believe a word of it. But here's the other thing. Malcolm is also – as you would hope from a best friend – nice. So he doesn't say to me, 'Bob, you're crazy.' He says, 'Wow, Bob, that's amazing.'

Maybe he thinks it's all a game. Perhaps he thinks it's my way of coping with losing Mum. Or maybe he thinks I'm bonkers, but doesn't really care.

It's confusing. But nobody said being a time traveller was easy.

'Remember that stuff I told you about time travelling?' I say now.

Malcolm nods.

'I know you don't believe it.'

'How did you know tha—' says Malcolm. 'I mean, of course I believe you.'

'It's fine,' I tell him. 'I wouldn't believe me either. And I can't prove it right now, but one day you'll see it for yourself. I've done this whole garage thing before.

That's how I knew Gloria was coming. And I've just been to the year 2043, where – by the way – you have really cool tattoos.'

Malcolm thinks about this for a few seconds. He frowns, and then he smiles.

'Awesome,' he says. 'I've always wanted tattoos. Maybe that's what I should do for a job.'

I think about telling him he already does – or will – but he'll figure it out for himself in good time.

'So,' says Malcolm. 'Earlier. What was that you were muttering about zombies?'

'I'm not entirely sure. But it seems the future has some sort of a zombie problem.'

'Awesome,' says Malcolm.

At the mention of zombies, a shiver runs up my back and the dark garage feels cold and spooky. I give the door a shove and it swings up and open. Sunlight floods into the dusty space, making bright spots and weird shapes blossom on my eyes.

When I blink them away, I am standing nose to nose with Gloria Dismal.

'I knew it,' she says, hands on hips, head tilted to one side like we've somehow disappointed her. 'What are you two doing lurking about in the dark?'

'We're not lurking, we're practising.'

And then someone laughs.

'Eno,' I say under my breath.

He is at the top of the driveway, sitting astride his ridiculous bicycle and looking – as ever – fantastically pleased with himself.

'I wouldn't waste my time practising if I were you,' says Eno. 'Everybody knows I'm going to win Griffin's Got Talent. The rest of you are there to –'

'Yeah, yeah,' I say, interrupting, 'to witness your greatness and a whole lot of other blah.'

Eno looks a little less sure of himself all of a sudden. And it feels good to see him lost for words. Especially because I took those words right out of his mouth.

'Go on,' I say. 'Scram. And quickly. Before Gloria throws something at you.'

I sense Gloria tensing beside me as if ready for action.

Eno smirks. He always smirks. But this is a particularly smirky smirk. 'You won't be smiling tomorrow,' he says. 'Oh no.'

And he pedals off out of sight.

And before he can pedal back into sight, I pull the garage door closed.

'Thank goodness he's gone,' says Gloria, removing her helmet and shaking loose her curly hair. She walks into the garage and flops down in Dad's wheelbarrow. 'Now, tell me all about this time-travelling zombie thing.'

Gloria has a range of head tilts. She has one for when she's thinking, another for listening, one for when she agrees, one for when she doesn't and one for when she hasn't made her mind up yet. She has a friendly head tilt, and a tilt for when she thinks you're being silly. The one she's tilting now is the one she uses when she's waiting for an answer and won't go away until she gets one.

'I don't know what you're talking about,' I say.

'It's you two that were talking about it,' says Gloria. '"Time travel", you said. "The future has a zombie problem," you said.'

'We were just . . . making stuff up.'

Gloria tilts her head to the opposite side. The I don't believe you side. 'I've had my suspicions about you, Robert Trebor.'

'Suspicions? What suspicions?'

'Ever since I heard you screaming in the bath, I thought to myself, there's something odd about that boy.'

'You heard what?'

'Thin walls,' says Gloria. 'I hear a lot.'

My tummy rumbles.

'And I certainly heard that.' She reaches into her massive bag. 'Luckily for you, I have —'

'Bananas,' I say, while her arm is still buried in the depths of her bag.

Gloria gives me a sideways glance and slowly removes four, slightly brown bananas. 'How did you know?'

I shrug. My tummy gurgles.

'Here,' says Gloria, lobbing a banana across the room. Her aim is terrible and Schnitzel has to duck to avoid being walloped in the face with a piece of over-ripe fruit.

'Dismal!'

'Oopsy.' She selects another and boomerangs it in my direction. It bounces off my drum and I snatch it out of the air.

'Boom,' says Gloria, as if she had intended the unlikely shot.

She reaches into her bag. Again.

'And don't even think about getting your tambourine out.'

Gloria Dismal freezes. Her eyes narrow. And – slowly – she pulls the tambourine from her bag.

'You knew,' she says. And it's not a question. 'You knew exactly what was in my bag.'

I try to smile innocently, but it's something I've never been very good at.

Gloria hops out of the wheelbarrow and rattles her tambourine at me. 'Explain yourself, future boy.'

'There's nothing to explain.'

'Don't believe you,' says Dismal, rattling her tambourine.

'Will you please stop rattling that thing in my face?'

'But this is the tambourine of truth,' says Dismal.

'Get away from me,' I say, holding up my banana for protection.

'It rattles when you lie,' says the Dismal One, giving the tambourine another jiggle. 'Now tell me about this time-travel nonsense. Tell me about these zombies.'

'There is no time travel.'

'Shake-a-shake-a,' says Gloria, advancing towards me with her tambourine.

And then I get the tingles. I get the drags. Everything goes fuzzy.

'Be right back,' I say, my voice sounding like it's underwater.

And I'm gone.

I don't even get a bite of my banana.

SELFIE ZOMBIES.
SMART WOOD.
A DISAPPOINTING TENNIS RACKET.
THE FATE OF ALL HUMANITY.

Malcolm and Future Me are wearing sunglasses and cycling helmets.

Future Me's helmet is designed to look like Iron Man's head. It's kind of cool. Well, it would be on an eleven-year-old, or even a fourteen-year-old, but on my thirty-one-year-old self, it looks utterly ridiculous.

Right now, though, this is not my main concern. My main concern is Malcolm.

He is screaming.

'Get back,' says Malcolm, waving a short wooden

cylinder at me. 'I'm not afraid to use this!'

The cylinder is about the size of a small can of pop. It doesn't look particularly dangerous.

'Hello, Bob,' says Future Bob.

'Bob?' says Malcolm. 'Bob!'

He presses a button on the cylinder and – with a whir and click – it extends into a full-sized wooden baseball bat.

'Cool bat,' I say.

'Yeah,' says Future Me. 'Smart wood. They make some lovely furniture. The chairs mould perfectly to the shape of your bum.'

'Ahem,' says Malcolm. 'A boy just materialised in the middle of the hallway. That's not normal. That's not even possible!'

He continues to point the baseball bat in my direction, staring wild-eyed and behaving as if he's never seen anybody appear out of thin air before. Which, in this timeline, he hasn't.

'Malcolm,' says Future Me, 'relax. I can explain.'

'Explain a child – who looks suspiciously like you used to, by the way – just appearing out of thin air?'

'Not exactly out of thin air,' says Future Me.

'Out of the past,' says me me.

Malcolm puts his free hand to his face. 'It's that time-travel thing you used to talk about, isn't it?'

'That's right.'

'Like that time in the garage with Gloria and the bananas?'

'Just like that,' says Future Me. 'Look, I know it's a lot to wrap your head around, and when this is all over – when everything is back to something like normal – I'll do my best to explain. But for now . . . can you just trust me?'

'That you're a time traveller?'

'Yes.'

'That the rules of the known physical universe don't apply to you?'

'That's about the long and short of it.'

Schnitzel considers. He looks from one of us to the other. Considers a bit more, then shrugs. He doesn't even ask if we're evil. And it seems to me that it's been slightly easier to convince him this time around. As if some deeply buried part of him is getting used to the idea.

'OK,' says Malcolm. 'Fair enough.'

'So,' I say to my future self, 'what did I miss?'

'Not much. I'm still planning on getting engaged, we still have zombies, and this one' – he flicks his eyes towards Malcolm – 'just dropped the banana bread again. Had real bananas in it this time, too.'

'Again?' says Malcolm.

'It's a time-loop kind of thing,' says Future Me.

'Right,' says Malcolm, frowning as if his brain is turning somersaults inside his skull.

'Wait a minute,' I say. 'How come he dropped it? It's not like I appeared in the kitchen this time.'

'Saw a spider,' he says with a great shoulder-shaking shudder. 'Huge thing.'

'Of course,' I say. Although there's nothing of course about it. It just feels like the right thing to say. 'So now what?'

Future Me checks his watch, and I notice it's one of those Mickey Mouse watches, where Mickey's hands move around to tell the time. I almost comment on it, but I'm not sure what I'd say.

'Now,' says Future Me. 'We get to the shops, buy more – very expensive – bananas and bake another – very expensive – banana bread.'

'Wait,' I say. 'Last time I was here, you said the world had been overrun with zombies?'

'That's right,' says Future Me. 'But don't worry, it'll be fine.'

He says 'fine' as if the world has been overrun with cute furry animals. Not flesh-eating zombies.

'It's not as if they're flesh-eating zombies,' he says.

'They're not brain-munching, tear-you-limb-from-limb zombies. They're selfie zombies.'

'What's a selfie zombie?'

'You know what selfies are?' says Future Me.

'Of course I do, I'm a child of the digital generation. Or at least that's what the teachers keep telling us.'

'So you know what selfie sticks are? Well, in the future, we have smile-activated selfie hats.'

'So your phone can always be in front of your face,' says Malcolm. 'You don't even need to press a button. Just say cheese and – click – the camera does the rest. Takes your picture, digitally removes the stupid selfie hat, makes your smile look bigger and brighter, then posts it to all of your social media sites. InstaGrin, Chatter, TipTop, all that nonsense.'

'The future is weird,' I say.

'Agreed,' says Future Me. 'And now more than ever. People have become seriously addicted to the selfie hat.'

'How do you get addicted to a . . . a hat?'

'Well, not so much the hat as their phones.'

'The way people in the past were addicted to nicotine not cigarettes,' says Malcolm.

'The hat is just the delivery system,' says Future Me. 'People were wearing them all day long – wore them to work, to the gym, to restaurants. Some people even slept in them. Hours and hours of screen time.'

'Then, about three months ago, we started seeing the first zombies,' says Malcolm.

'So why not just take their hats off them?' I ask.

Future Me shakes his head. 'You'd have more luck trying to take a banana off a gorilla.'

'Besides,' says Malcolm, 'something had happened at a deep, neural level.'

I nod like I have even the faintest idea what this means.

'The software manipulated the plasticity of the users' cerebral architecture,' says Future Me. 'And likewise, the reorganised nervous system retro-coded the software for instant retinal transmission.'

I stop nodding. 'In English please?'

'It messed up their brains,' says Malcolm.

'And weaponised their phones.'

'Selfie zombies are interested in two things,' says Future Me. 'Talking selfies and making more selfie zombies.'

'How do they make more zombies?' I ask.

'A couple of ways,' says Malcolm.

'Taking your picture, mainly,' says Future Me. 'So if one of those things comes near you, don't – whatever you do – look into their camera.'

'You said there were two ways.'

Future Me and Future Malcolm exchange glances.

'What?'

'Well,' says Future Me, 'if they can't take your picture, they tend to get a bit . . . bitey.'

'Bitey? I thought you said they weren't flesh-eating zombies.'

'That's right. They don't actually eat anything, just, you know, bite.'

'And all of this because some egghead invented a selfie hat? What kind of maniac would do something like that?'

'You go to school with him,' says Malcolm.

'Not you?'

Malcolm laughs. 'I can't even get my toaster to work properly.'

'I thought you worked with nanobots?'

'Nanobots are easy compared to toasters.'

I find this highly unlikely, but now is not the time to get into it. 'So who's the maniac?'

'Eno Fezzinuff,' says Future Me.

'Eno? You have got to be kidding!'

'Wish I was. It would save both of us a lot of bother.'

'Bother? Both of us? What's any of this got to do with me?'

'You have to go back to the past, Bob. Change the

course of history and save civilisation from an outbreak of selfie zombies.'

'Why me? Why do I have to save civilisation?'

'Know any other time travellers?'

I shake my head sulkily.

'Exactly,' says Future Me. 'If it helps, just think of it as an exciting homework project.'

'No,' I say, 'that does not help one bit, Mr Trebor. For one, there is no such thing as "exciting homework", and for two, if there was, it would almost certainly not involve zombies.'

'Come on, Bob. What could be more grown-up than saving the world?'

Future Me looks at me and smiles. He waits. The way grown-ups do. When they know full well you're going to do something. Even if you don't want to. It's really annoying.

'Fine,' I say. 'Fine. I'll save the world.'

'Excellent,' says Future Me.

'One thing,' I say.

Future Me raises an eyebrow: What?

'How?'

'Oh, that's easy,' says Future Me. 'All you have to do is win Griffin's Got Talent.'

'Wait. You're telling me we don't?'

Future Me rolls up his coat sleeve to reveal – just above the Mickey Mouse watch – a weird lump on his hairy forearm.

'What's that?'

'We broke our wrist the night before the competition.'

'No! Ouch! How?'

'Slipped on Gloria's skateboard,' he says, with something like a fond smile.

'I knew she was trouble.'

'Let's not get hung up on that,' says Future Me. 'The point is, with the Tentacles of Time out of the way, Eno won Griffin's Got Talent with his –'

'Don't tell me. With his smile-activated selfie hat.'

'Bingo,' says Future Me. 'The win inspired him, then blah blah blah next thing you know Eno's an evil genius and responsible for the downfall of modern society.'

'You don't think, perhaps you've "blah blah blah" jumped to a few conclusions?'

Future Me wanders over to a bookshelf and picks up a thick hardback. 'It's all here in his autobiography.'

On the cover is a man with dark hair, thick eyebrows and a smirk that suggests he's rather pleased with himself. Even without reading the name on the cover, it's undeniably Eno. The book's title is: *Enough Is Not Fezzinuff: The autobiography of a genius*.

'Modest,' I say.

Future Me laughs. 'Well, now you have a chance to go back in time, make sure it never happens, and save the future of humanity while you're at it.'

'No pressure, then?'

It's meant to sound sarcastic, but either I'm doing it wrong or Future Me doesn't notice.

'That's the spirit,' he says. 'Now let's get you kitted up. I've got your old skateboard helmet somewhere.'

Future Me pulls open the hallway cupboard and rummages around until he finds what he's looking for.

'How about that,' he says, pushing my helmet onto my head. 'Still fits.'

'Of course it still fits. I only got it two weeks ago.'

Future Me picks up a wooden cylinder from a shelf by the door, similar to the one Malcolm was brandishing earlier, and drops it into his pocket.

'I'm afraid I don't have a smart bat for you,' he says, handing me a tennis racket, 'but this should do the trick.'

'You are joking?'

'What's wrong with it?'

'It's a tennis racket,' I say. 'And half the strings are busted. It's hardly any good for bashing zombies' brains in, is it?'

'Who said anything about bashing brains in?' says Malcolm.

'They're zombies, aren't they? What else are you supposed to do?'

'Zombies have rights too,' says Malcolm.

I swish my tennis racket through the air. 'What's this for, then?'

'Prodding,' says Malcolm, making a nudging motion with his baseball bat.

'Just . . . you know, nudge them out of the way,' says Future Me.

'Brilliant,' I say. 'Just brilliant.'

'Are you trying to do sarcasm?' says Malcolm.

'Maybe.'

'Ah,' says the man who used to be my best friend, 'that's cute.'

'Right,' says Future Me, 'enough talking, let's get bananas.'

He opens the front door, and we step out into the zombie-infested future.

7

CROWDED SKIES.
A BIKE RIDE BY MOONLIGHT.
DIRTY FINGERNAILS AND BAD BREATH.
SMIIIIIIILE!

It was a bright afternoon when I was yanked out of my garage and dumped into the future. But when we step outside Future Me's front door, the last of the daylight is fading and there's a chill in the air. I shiver. But that might just be the idea that there are zombies out here somewhere.

'Lovely night for a bike ride,' says Future Me.

'Bike ride!' I say. 'Wouldn't it make more sense to take a car?'

Malcolm's bike is leaning against our front wall. He goes over to it and swings his leg over the crossbar.

'Actually,' says Future Me, 'we call them all-terrain electric craft.'

'All terrain? Like . . . underwater?'

Malcolm nods, He glances upwards. 'And . . . up there.'

'You're kidding? You have flying cars now?'

'Craft,' says Malcolm. 'We call them craft.'

I look up to the sky and it's dotted with lights, some whizzing by just above the rooftops, but more above and beyond.

'They're all craft?' I ask.

'Drones too,' says Malcolm. 'Delivery drones, repair drones, police drones.'

'Ice-cream drones,' says Future Me.

My tummy rumbles.

'But not at this time of night,' he says, reading my mind.

'So where's your craft?' I ask my future self.

'Don't have one.'

'What! You live in the future – a future with flying cars – and you ride a bike!'

'I find riding a bicycle keeps me connected with my inner child,' says Future Me.

'Ahem,' I say, pointing at myself. 'Speaking as your inner child, I would much prefer a flying car. Honestly, being grown-up is wasted on adults.'

'Don't be in such a hurry to grow up,' says my future self.

'You sound like Dad.'

'Well,' says Future Me, 'maybe he and I are both right. Come on.'

Future Me raises the garage door, and what I see inside makes me gasp.

The garage is clean and well lit. On shelves and in boxes are all kinds of toys and games from . . . well, my childhood. My pogo stick, my rubber-sucker bow and arrow, my whoopee cushion and games console. There are board games, a remote-controlled car, a Captain America costume and shield. All clean, shining and neatly displayed. There is other stuff, too, that I haven't seen before; stuff that must belong to older versions of myself: a punch bag, a skateboard, a dart board. A collection of baseball caps. Shelves of comics and books.

It's like a museum to my childhood – the part I've already lived and the part that's waiting for me, out there in the future.

'It's awesome,' I say. 'Totally and utterly awesome. But . . . what's it all about?'

Future Me taps his chest, just above his heart. 'It's good for the inner child,' he says. 'Plus, who knows when some younger version of myself might turn up and need . . . oh, I dunno, the Machine of Ultimate Velocity.'

And there in the corner of the garage is the bike I got

for my ninth birthday. It's a bit small for me now, my knees come up to my chin when I'm pedalling, but it's still a wicked ride. And it's in better condition now than it was the last time I rode it. The paintwork is perfect and unchipped, the chrome sparkles, even the rip in the saddle has been repaired.

I climb on and ding the bell. It sounds good.

Future Me grabs his own bike and together we roll our rides towards the garage entrance and . . .

'You're kidding me.'

'What?' says Future Me. 'What's the matter?'

'Flat tyre,' I say.

'Two by the looks of it,' says Malcolm, giving the back wheel a pinch.

Future Me shakes his head. 'Sorry, Bob. Keeping on top of this lot is a full-time job.'

'So now what?'

'Only one thing for it,' says my future self. 'Jump on the back. I'll give you a seater.'

The streets are familiar but different at the same time.

The lampposts from twenty years ago have vanished; in their place a row of disc-shaped lights hover above the pavements like a fleet of tiny, glowing UFOs. Although several of these appear to be broken – flickering, fizzing or simply not working.

Craft float in driveways where cars once stood. But for vehicles so futuristic, they look old and unloved. Dirty windscreens, dented doors, scratched paintwork.

The houses, too, look neglected. The buildings themselves haven't changed much – they are still made of brick, still attached to the ground – but the gardens are overgrown and many of the windows are covered with nailed-on wooden boards.

There are potholes in the road and piles of rotting rubbish on the pavements.

'What happened to the place?' I say.

'Zombies happened,' says Future Me.

'People are afraid to go out,' says Malcolm.

'And with so many infected,' Future Me continues, 'there aren't enough people to do all the jobs that make the world go around.'

'Teachers, dentists, bin-men, builders and so on,' says Malcolm.

I shrug. 'Less teachers I can live with. Dentists, too.'

'Also, most of the shops have closed down. No more bakery, no pizzeria, no sweet shop,' says Future Me.

'Nooooo!' I shout into the night. And because it's so awful, I shout it again.

'I know,' says Future Me. 'But you can fix it, Bob. You can fix the future.'

We ride in silence for a while, moving through the deserted streets, past derelict buildings, abandoned cars and worrying shadows.

After ten minutes or so, Future Me steers his bike towards the park and there is a faint sound of moaning in the air. Perhaps it's the wind blowing through the trees. Except, there doesn't appear to be any wind. And there aren't any trees. I clutch my tennis racket in one fist, and with my other arm tighten my hold around Future Me's waist.

Again, something moans on the wind. Future Me must hear it too because he stops pedalling.

Malcolm does the same, both bikes rolling slowly to a halt.

We're outside the old playground, and as far as I can tell, it hasn't changed at all in the last twenty years – same roundabout, same climbing-frame and slide.

The swings creak as they rock gently back and forth. And again, I shiver.

Future Me steps off the bike and steadies it while I hop off the back. He points to the far end of the park, to a dark shape that looks like some kind of wild, scraggly bush. It's a mess of skinny twigs and strange square leaves.

'What is it?' I whisper.

'Zed cluster,' says Malcolm, coming over to join us.

'A what?'

'Bunch of zombies,' says Future Me, and my heart leaps.

As I watch, the thing I mistook for a hedge shifts, and I can make out the shapes of tightly packed bodies.

'What are those things sticking up out of it?'

'Selfie hats,' says Future Me.

'What are they doing?'

'What do you think they're doing?' says Malcolm. 'They're taking selfies.'

'In a park? At night?'

'What can I tell you?' says Future Me. 'They're selfie zombies.'

And in the distance, I see the glow of the phone screens now. I hear the click, click, click of the cameras above the low moan of maybe twenty zombies.

'Can we sneak past them?'

'Possibly,' says Future Malcolm. 'But where there's

one cluster, there's usually more. Best to steer clear.'

'So what's the plan?'

'Back on the bikes,' says Future Me. 'We'll go around the park and head through the underpass.'

'The underpass?'

'It's a footpath that runs under the main road,' Malcolm says.

'I know what an underpass is, Malcolm. It just sounds like exactly the sort of place a zombie would hang out.'

'We'll cross that bridge when we get to it,' says Future Me.

'I thought it was an underpass,' I say.

'It's a figure of speech,' says Future Me.

'What is? The bridge bit or the underpass bit?'

'Can we just get moving?' says Future Me, climbing onto the bike.

I hop up behind him and wrap my arm around his waist.

Then someone else wraps their arm around my waist.

It's a very strong arm.

The hand is dirty and its fingernails are long and black with muck.

I catch a whiff of foul breath on the breeze.

I scream.

And then we're all screaming, and I'm trying to get off the bike but I'm trapped between my future self and whatever it is that has its filthy arm wrapped around me. In the muddle, Future Me loses his balance and the three of us tumble to the ground.

The zombie has landed in a sitting position, but seems in no immediate hurry to move. Wrapped around her forehead is a wide headband and attached to the front of this is a short bendy stick, like a child's fishing rod, and dangling from the end, swaying gently from the fall, is a phone. The zombie smiles, the phone flashes.

The creature is both ridiculous and terrifying, and I can't tear my eyes away from it.

'Remember. Don't look at the camera!' shouts Future Me.

The zombie shows its teeth in a hideous skull-like grin. 'Smiiiiile,' it whispers, and its breath smells of bad meat, feet and dirty laundry. 'Smmmmiile.'

The zombie stretches its arms towards me. It moves slowly, and I really should get the heck out of here, but I'm frozen to the spot, as if hypnotised by the dangling phone, the hideous grin, the grasping hands, the long filthy fingernails . . .

A moment before the zombie grabs me, someone takes hold of me beneath the armpits and yanks me to my feet.

The zombie snaps her teeth and a thick gob of drool spills over her bottom lip.

'Looks like we've got a biter,' says Future Me. 'Get behind me!'

He pulls his smart bat from his pocket and pushes the button.

Nothing happens.

He pushes the button again. Several times. Still nothing.

'Is it stuck?' I ask.

'I forgot to charge it,' he says with an apologetic shrug. 'Oh well.'

'You dope!'

'Sorreee for not being perfect.'

I'm about to point out that I don't need perfect, what I need is a better weapon than a tennis racket and a flat smart bat to protect myself against a foul-smelling selfie zombie. But then the foul-smelling selfie zombie makes my point for me with a single word.

'Smiiiiiiiile,' says the selfie zombie, saliva glistening on her horrible gnashers.

'Smiiiile,' says a whole group of voices, as if in answer.

And it seems our new friend is not alone. Over her shoulder, a group of five or six zombies emerges from the shadows, all wearing selfie hats, all staring straight at us.

GRADUAL ATTACK OF THE SELFIE ZOMBIES.
NANOBOT FREAKOUT.
PRETTY MUCH DOOMED.
A BOOT IN THE BACK.

'In here!' says Future Me, opening the gate to the playground.

Future Me sees me safely through, then follows with Malcolm close behind.

'Don't forget to shut the gate,' says Future Me.

'Oops,' says Malcolm, but as he turns, the first zed is shuffling into the playground.

And on its heels, the rest of the zombies come

staggering behind, teeth bared, phones bobbing, cameras clicking.

'This way!' shouts Malcolm, and he heads directly for the roundabout.

'Too exposed,' Future Me says. 'We should head for high ground. Up the slide!'

More zombies have arrived now, all of them making their way into the playground. All of them coming for us. They're slow. But they're still, you know, zombies.

'I dunno,' says Malcolm. 'The slide is high, and I admit that's an attractive feature. But the roundabout goes round, you see, creating a moving target and allowing for a swift exit should one be needed.'

'Good point,' says Future Me, scratching his chin. 'It's a tough call.'

Every few steps, the zombies stop, huddle together, and smile for a group selfie. Even so, they are gradually closing in on us.

As well as their rotten teeth and filthy nails, some of the zombies have scratches on their skin, one has a clump of hair pulled out, another shuffles forward on what appears to be a broken leg. They are – in a word – horrifying.

'What happened to them?' I say.

'They're too busy taking selfies to take care of themselves,' says Future Me.

'Not brushing your teeth is one thing,' I say. 'But they look like they've been in a war.'

'They do play rough,' says Future Me.

'Are you sure she's worth it?' I say. 'This . . .' I can barely say the word '. . . girlfriend.'

A dreamy look passes across my future face. 'Absolutely, totally and utterly,' he says. 'I can't imagine life without her.'

'It's your life I'm worried about,' I say. 'We're surrounded by about forty zombies here.'

The zombie with the broken leg limps towards

us. Her face is twisted in what could be pain, hunger, determination, or all three.

'Right,' says Future Me. 'Decision time. Hands up for the roundabout.'

Malcolm puts his hand up.

The zombies shamble forward.

'OK,' says Future Me, 'that's one for the roundabout. Now, who's for the slide?'

Future Me reaches his own hand into the air, going up on tiptoes as he does it, as if this extra height will carry the vote. He looks at me, as if urging me to take his side. The whole thing is ridiculous.

'OK, one apiece,' says my future self. 'Bob, you have the deciding vote. Slide or roundabout? Or would you prefer something else? The monkey bars, perhaps?'

'What I would prefer,' I say, 'is not to be grabbed, scratched or bitten by a smelly zombie.'

'Relax,' says Future Me, 'there's plenty of . . . oh . . . oh bum.'

'Yes,' I say. 'Bum.'

In the time – the very long time – that me and Future Me and Malcolm have been debating whether to take shelter on the roundabout or the slide, the zombies have finally closed in. They're close enough to smell now, close enough that I can see the bloodshot veins in their eyes, and almost – almost – close enough to touch.

My future best friend hops onto the roundabout.

Big Bob takes me by the hand and pulls me through a gap in the gathering circle of zombies. They may be slow moving, but what they lack in speed they make up for in numbers – there are dozens of them. We make it to the monkey bars, but the ground on either side is thick with zombies.

'We'll have to make like monkeys,' says Future Me. And he jumps up, grabs the closest bar and sets off swinging.

It's a bigger jump for me, but I make it by the tips of my fingers.

'This is harder than I remember,' says Future Me, pausing halfway to catch his breath.

I look over my shoulder and, to my absolute horror, see that one of the zombies has jumped up behind us.

'Move,' I say to Future Me. 'We've got company.'

Future Me picks up the pace and makes it to the end of the bars before his grip gives out. He drops to the ground and yelps in pain.

I drop down neatly beside him. 'You OK?'

'Twisted my knee,' he says. 'But I'll live.'

Not if we don't keep moving, I think.

The playground is crowded with the shuffling, smiling zombies by now. Some are distracted by the playground equipment (one is taking a selfie on the wobbly giraffe, and two more are taking selfies on the swings), but most of the zombies are much more interested in us. Like the one behind us, moving steadily along the monkey bars.

'Put your arm around my shoulder,' I say, and me
and my future self hobble onwards.

We're almost at the slide, but the quickest way is
blocked by a huddle of zombies.

'We'll have to go over the balance beam,' I say. 'Can
you make it?'

'Only one way to find out.'

Future Me steps one foot onto the beam, then the other – he wobbles, but his balance holds. I climb up behind him and we begin inching our way forward. We're almost across, when a humongous zombie climbs up onto the other end of the beam and begins creeping towards us.

'Smiiiiile,' says the zombie.

'Not today,' says Future Me.

The balance beam passes alongside a sandpit, and Future Me half jumps, half falls directly into its centre. He yells in pain as he lands.

And now, the zombie jumps down too.

The two face each other and it looks like things are going to end badly, but Future Me has a surprise in store. He grabs a small plastic bucket, scoops up a load of sand and hurls it at the teenaged zombie. Probably, he just meant to throw the sand, but the bucket flies from his hand and clocks the zombie high on his forehead. The zombie staggers backwards, trips over his own feet and lands on his bottom in the sandpit. Future Me grabs me by the hand and together we run and limp the last few steps to the slide.

We make it up the ladder in a handful of seconds, and take cover inside the wooden den at the top. The ground around us is quickly covered with moaning, grinning zombies. One of them wraps a hand around a rung on the ladder, but when he goes to grab another rung, the dangling phone gets in his way; he loses his grip and falls back into the mob, toppling them into a heap.

For the moment we're safe. But sooner or later the zombies will figure out a way of getting to us.

'I used to love this place,' says Future Me. 'Do you still come here? I can't remember.'

I pull a face. 'Are you serious? I'm in big school now. I haven't been here since I was ten!'

'Shame,' says Future Me. 'We used to love the swings. You know, I think I'm going to come back here when there're no zombies and have a good old play. You should too.'

'You can act like a child if you like, but don't expect me to.'

He shakes his head sadly. 'Don't wish your youth away, Bob. Because, unfortunately, the day will come – and quicker than you think – when you really are too old for a playground. When your bones ache at the mere idea of jumping off a swing or hanging upside down from the monkey bars.'

I roll my eyes.

'It's important, Bob. Trust me.'

I'm about to explain to my future self that it's difficult to trust a man who drags you into a night full of zombies armed with nothing more than a tennis racket, but a loud yell snaps our attention to the roundabout.

Malcolm is on board and spinning fast, but he is surrounded by zombies. He clutches onto the rail with one hand and swings his bat with the other. Wallop!

He hits a phone and sends it flying from its owner's silly hat.

'Yaaah!' he shouts, and he swings again, this time clobbering a zombie around the head.

'Sorry!' Malcolm yells. 'My bad!'

He steps one leg off the platform now, and uses it to power the roundabout into a faster spin. He swings again and again, sending phones and selfie hats sailing into the moonlight. The zombies, separated from their precious devices, lurch off looking to reclaim their phones. Or – judging by the scuffling and snarling – any phone whatsoever.

I punch the air and shout, 'Go Malcolm!'

As he swings his bat again, my old friend releases his other hand from the rail and gives me a thumbs up.

Big mistake.

Without a grip on the rapidly rotating roundabout, Malcolm wobbles, staggers and is thrown straight into the clutches of three zombies.

They swarm over him, wrap their arms around his shoulders and pull him into their hideous embrace. Cameras click and flash as the zombies take selfie after selfie with Malcolm.

Eyes screwed shut, Malcolm fights to free himself – but there are too many of them. One of the zombies grabs his head and another attempts to peel open his left eyelid.

'Aaarghhh!' screams Malcolm. 'My eyes, they're going for my eyes!'

'I told him the roundabout was a bad idea,' says Future Me.

'Smiiiiiiiile,' moan the zombies. 'Smiiiiiiiiiiiiiiile.'

As well as the zombies working on Malcolm's eyes, others are now attached to his arms and legs, each pulling in a different direction. I can see now why they all look so beaten up – this isn't just playing 'rough', this is playing downright deadly.

The zombie latched onto Malcolm's right leg is a big

fella and he is pulling hard. Malcolm's leg is stretched out completely as the zombie leans back, loading all of his considerable weight against Malcolm. There is a loud ripping sound followed by a sickening pop, followed by the Schnitzel screaming. The zombie holding his leg goes reeling backwards as something comes loose.

'His leg!' I yelp. 'They took his leg!'

'Boot,' says my future self. 'They took his boot.'

I remove my hands from my eyes and see that Malcolm's leg is still attached to his body. The zombie is chewing Malcolm's boot, either not aware or not caring that there's no foot inside it.

Malcolm is still fighting the zombies; one stripy sock is exposed and his yellow underpants are showing through a split in his jeans. Which, I guess, explains the ripping sound.

As Malcolm attempts to fight off the zombies, his hair turns from brown to blue to red to green – standing up, twisting, frizzing and curling at random. His tattoos flash on and off, showing hearts, snakes, daggers, octopuses, scrolls and skulls.

'What's happening?'

'His nanobots are malfunctioning,' says Future Me. 'Must be the stress.'

He gives me a strange look then, a worrying look, but I don't have time to think or ask about it. More zombies swarm around Malcolm, they grab at him with their grubby hands, they press their stinking faces up against his, and as they crowd closer my best friend vanishes from view.

A scream rises up from the tangled knot of bodies.

And then everything falls quiet.

'Do you think he's OK?' I say.

'I very much doubt it,' says Future Me.

The huddle of bodies begins to move and separate, and there, in the centre, is Malcolm. His T-shirt is ripped, there are scratch marks on his arms and neck and his head is twisted at an uncomfortable angle.

His hair stands in stiff green spikes and a single tattoo flashes on and off across his forehead. It reads:

SMILE!

My best friend is a zombie.

Malcolm points to me and Future Me at the top of the slide, and then – his voice a dry, creepy croak – he says aloud the word that is written across his head. 'Smiiiile.'

'They're coming for us!' I yelp. 'Bob, they're coming for us!'

The zombies are gathering around the base of the slide, some trying to climb the slippery metal chute. One is making slow progress towards us, and given enough time he will reach the den.

'Looks like we're pretty much doomed,' says my annoying future self.

'Maybe we could hold out until their phones run out of battery?'

Future Me laughs. 'Built-in solar-powered, lunar-powered, voice-powered, movement-powered energy packs. Those things last years.'

'Right,' I say. 'So much for that idea.'

'I'd prepare myself for a rather unpleasant zombie mauling, if I were you. Which – now that I think about it – I am,' says Future Me. 'Or was. It gets confusing.'

'Are you trying to terrify me?' I say.

'Have you ever wondered what brings the tingles

on?' he asks. 'Why the drags happen when they happen?' And he gives me that look again, the one he flashed at me while Malcolm was malfunctioning.

'Of course I have.'

'Stress,' says Future Me.

The lead zombie is now halfway up the slide. A shiver races up my back, my feet itch, the palms of my hands prickle.

'You're telling me I travel when I'm stressed?'

'It's a theory,' says Future Me.

'You mean you don't know?'

'Not yet,' says Future Me, and the goon shoves me down the slide.

I try to clutch the sides, but this is – always was – a slippery slide, and I'm slowly but steadily going down. And the climbing zombie is steadily coming up.

My skin starts to creep and crawl and prickle.

'Getting the tingles?' asks my hateful future self. 'Or have we moved on to the drags yet?'

And there it is – the feeling of being squashed and squeezed and generally roughed up by a large octopus with powerful tentacles.

'Save the world, Bob. History will thank you!'

'I hate you!' I shout.

The zombie stretches a hand towards me.

I'm too young to be a zombie, I like my arms and legs attached and – a terrible thought occurs to me . . .

What if I get zombified then ping back in time and start a zombie apocalypse in 2023?! I'd be in so much trouble. I'm about to say exactly this when Future Me puts his boot in my back.

'And don't break your wrist,' he says, before giving me a final shove.

I scream.

The drags take me.

And I'm gone.

The Sad Bit

Stress, Future Me said, might be the trigger that sends me travelling through time. He's been time travelling for a lot longer than I have, so perhaps he has a point.

This latest trip, for example, started with Gloria Dismal shaking a tambourine in my face. Not the most stressful experience, you might think, but it was also the day before GGT.

Also also, I had Eno being all smug and boasty at the top of my driveway.

So, yeah, you could certainly say I was stressed.

I was stressed the first time too.

Although stress doesn't seem a big enough word for the way I was feeling that day. The day after my eleventh birthday. The day after Mum died.

And it was all my fault.

What I wanted for my eleventh birthday was one of those fitness-tracking, step-counting Bluetooth smart watches. I mean, who doesn't want to know how many steps they've taken in a day? Exactly. So that's what I asked for.

When I came downstairs on the morning of my birthday, there was a pile of neatly wrapped presents sitting on the kitchen table. My eye went immediately to the smallest of these. A neat oblong package, just about the perfect size to hold, oh I dunno, a digital watch, maybe?

I tore open the wrapping paper (stars, moons, comets) to reveal a plain brown cardboard box. Malcolm's watch came in a silver box with a picture of the watch on the front. This had nothing on it at all.

I hesitated. But then I looked at Mum's face – she looked excited and her eyes urged me on.

I opened the box. And stared at what was inside.

A Mickey Mouse watch with a bright red strap. It didn't even look new.

I looked at Mum and the disappointment must

have shown on my face. Because as I stared at her, Mum's smile faded and vanished.

'What's wrong?' she said.

'I wanted one that counts my steps,' I said.

'When you've walked enough, your legs get tired. You don't need some device to tell you that.'

'Everyone else has one.'

'So don't be everyone else,' Mum said. 'Be an individual.' She nodded towards the Mickey Mouse watch. 'I'll bet no one else has one of these.'

And I'll regret what I said next for the rest of my life.

'That's because it's babyish.'

Mum stared at me. 'No,' she said. 'It's your behaviour that's babyish.' And she walked out of the room.

Dad hadn't said a word up to this point. And he said nothing now. He just shook his head and followed Mum out of the room. I knew I was behaving like an ungrateful brat, but I was too embarrassed – too stubborn, I suppose – to admit it. So I sat on my own, still holding the watch, still surrounded by a pile of beautifully wrapped presents that I didn't deserve. Maybe I sat there for a minute, maybe it was ten, but when I finally plucked up the courage to go and apologise, Mum wasn't there.

'I'm sorry,' I said to Dad.

He ruffled my hair to show me that he still loved me. 'It's your mum you need to apologise to.'

'Where is she?'

'Went to the shops,' he said. 'You can tell her you're sorry when she comes home.'

But she never made it home. She never even made it to the shops.

A freak accident, apparently.

The details don't matter; all that matters is that it began with me.

That's what I was thinking about the next night while I sat – tired and tearful – in a bathtub of cooling water. I was wishing – wishing with every bit of belief

I had – that I could go back just one day. So I could be better. So I could put it right.

But it didn't work out that way.

Instead of going backwards, I went ten minutes in the opposite direction.

So, maybe Future Me's theory is right. Maybe that is the key.

But that still doesn't excuse the monkey-brained maniac for booting me down a slide into the clutches of a hoard of selfie zombies. And I will tell him as much next time I see him.

A DROPPED EGG.
HONESTY HURTS.
A WHEELBARROWFUL OF DISMAL.
A BROKEN WRIST HURTS MORE.

Time travel – as I understand it – which isn't much – is not exact.

Imagine swinging on a swing and, right when you're at the highest point, trying to drop an egg into a teacup. You might – if you're very skilful, or extremely lucky – hit the target. But most of the time, you're going to get egg all over the place.

Well, time travel is a bit like that. It's not exact. And when I bounce, I don't always return to the exact point at which I left. And if you're wondering why someone might be trying to chuck an egg into a teacup while riding the swings – well, people do all kinds of strange things. Don't worry about it.

I bounce back into the garage at the point where Dismal – still lounging in Dad's wheelbarrow – has her arm buried up to the elbow in the depths of her ridiculous bag. Again.

Judging by the look on her face, we are at the point where I have correctly predicted she is about to pull a tambourine from her bag. Gloria does exactly that, then gives the thing a shake.

'You knew,' she says. 'You knew exactly what was in my bag.'

'And you knew Gloria was coming,' says Malcolm.

I do my innocent smile again, but it's just as unconvincing as last time.

Gloria sits up, ready to climb out of the wheelbarrow.

'Stay where you are!' I say, pointing at her with the banana I just that moment realise I'm holding.

'Oooh,' says Dismal, 'you look just like a teacher when you get bossy.'

'Do not!!'

Schnitzel snorts with laughter and I flick him a fierce stare.

When Gloria Dismal gets an idea in her head, she's like a cat with a mouse in its mouth. There is no way she is letting go of it. Trying to hide what I am from her now would be a gigantic waste of time. And when it's your responsibility to save the world, time is not for wasting. So here goes nothing.

'I'm going to tell you something crazy,' I say. 'It's impossible, unbelievable and ridiculous. But I need you to trust me.'

'Oh, goody,' says Dismal, clapping her hands together, 'tell me more.'

'Fine,' I say. 'But there's something else I need to do first.' My tummy rumbles.

Gloria raises her eyebrows questioningly.

In answer, I peel the banana and take a huge bite. In a moment, my belly will thank me, but first my taste-buds do a little dance of joy inside my mouth. The banana is bruised, over-ripe, and a bit squishy. But it's real – an 'originana', as they say in the future – and it tastes amazing. I finish the banana with one more greedy chomp and shove the peel into my pocket where there's no chance of me slipping on it and breaking my wrist.

'Happy now?' says Dismal.

'More than you know,' I say through a mouthful of banana.

'Good,' says Dismal. 'Now talk.'

So I swallow my banana and I talk. I tell them everything, from the day I time travelled in my bathtub, right up to the point where my future self kicked me down a slide into the clutches of a zombie with bad breath.

Well, I tell them almost everything. I leave out the

bit about Malcolm being mangled and mauled by a pack of zombies. It would only give him bad dreams.

'So they were baking,' says Gloria, holding a banana and inspecting it as if it contains the answers to life, the universe and everything.

'That's not the important part,' I tell her. 'The important part is we have to win Griffin's Got Talent tomorrow to stop Eno Fezzinuff from becoming an evil genius and starting a zombie apocalypse.'

'What's an apopalips?' asks Malcolm.

'End of the world. Downfall of mankind. Destruction of the human race. Collapse of civilisation kind of thing.'

'Ah,' says Malcolm.

'Exactly. And to stop it happening, I need to make sure my wrists stay unbroken. So first things first, I need you, Gloria, to get your skateboard out of here.'

'Okey-doke,' says Gloria, and with one long leg she kicks her skateboard across the garage floor and out into the driveway. 'Now what?'

'Now, we practise,' I say. 'Like the future of the world depends on it.'

'Great,' says Gloria, who is still holding her tambourine. 'Where do you want me?'

I stare at her in disbelief. 'Are you serious?'

'Deadly,' she says. 'If the world needs saving, I want in.'

'Where I want you, Gloria, is at home. In your own house. So me and Malcolm can get our act together.'

'Thing is,' says Gloria, 'and don't take this the wrong way, but have you ever considered the possibility that the Tentacles of Time might – just possibly – be rubbish?'

I've been through a lot in the last few hours – I've travelled in time, discovered I am not famous, that I'm a history teacher with a girlfriend who I intend to marry, I've been chased by zombies and kicked down a slide by myself. But this . . . this is the limit!

'Get out!' I say, pointing to the garage door. 'And take your tambourine with you.'

'I'm trying to be helpful,' protests the Dismal One.

'And how exactly is telling us we're . . . rubbish helpful?'

'You said the fate of the world depended on you winning. Well, if that's true –'

'It is true,' I say, and my voice has gone all high and screechy.

'In whi--ch case,' says the Dismal One, 'I have a duty to be honest. And I don't see you winning GGT. Not without help, anyway.'

'Well, thank you so much for your honesty,' I say. 'You can go now.'

'You don't have a proper song,' says Dismal. 'Malcolm's guitar is missing a string.'

'Wonderful,' I say. 'The door's over there. Goodbye.'

'Also,' Dismal adds, 'drummers are meant to keep steady time. Which you don't. But me and my tambourine' – she taps the instrument against her free hand – 'do. And I'm working on a song. I think you'll like it.'

'Great,' I say. 'Why don't you go home and work on it. On your own.'

I get up from my drum kit and open the garage door. I point to the outside. 'This way please.'

Dismal doesn't move. She looks up at me from Dad's wheelbarrow with her big brown eyes. 'But I want to help.'

My words are having no effect on Gloria, so it's time to take action.

I pick up her bag, her various items of jumble and dump them on top of her. And then I grab the handles of the wheelbarrow and with a mighty heave begin rolling the lot towards the door.

I'm almost there when my foot lands on something soft and slippery. And I know before I see it that I have just stepped on the first of Dismal's flung bananas. The one that nearly whacked Malcolm in the face is now beneath my shoe.

My legs go from under me, I wobble, lurch and

topple. I reach out with my right hand, grasping at thin air in a desperate attempt to stop my fall, but it's useless, and as I crash sideways my hand hits the concrete floor and the sound of my wrist snapping is loud and clear and horrible. Pain shoots up my arm like electricity and my wrist is bent at a revoltingly unnatural angle.

I tell myself not to scream.

Myself doesn't listen.

Myself screams.

A RATHER OBVIOUS DIAGNOSIS.
CHOCOLATE ICE-CREAM.
ACTUALLY, IT COULD WELL BE THE END OF THE WORLD.
LIVE IN THE MOMENT.

'Open wide,' says Dad, and he feeds another spoonful of chocolate ice-cream into my mouth.

It's four hours later. We've done the panic, the questions, the drive to hospital, the X-ray, and the rather obvious diagnosis of two broken bones in my right wrist. And now we're sitting at the kitchen table sharing a bowl of ice-cream. The same table where, twenty years from now, I will sit around a smashed cake while my future self tells me about his plans to get married. It's enough to give you brain freeze.

'Are you sure you didn't do this just to avoid eating my broccoli and mackerel casserole?' Dad asks.

Dad's casserole is awful, but it's not so bad I'd deliberately break my arm to get out of eating it. Maybe a grazed knee, or a paper-cut, or some nettle rash would be worth it, but not a busted arm.

'I'm sure,' I tell him.

Dad stares at me hard, as if he's trying to decide whether or not I'm telling the truth. And then he smiles. He takes a spoonful for himself and scoops out one more for me.

'I'm not a baby,' I say.

'Son,' says Dad, 'you will always be my baby. No matter what age you are. And particularly when you're hurt.'

'I can eat with my left hand.'

'Not very well,' says Dad, nodding at the brown

stain on the front of my T-shirt. 'I guess you won't be drumming for a while.'

'Actually, I've been thinking about that. I reckon I could shove a drumstick down inside the cast.'

'No chance,' says Dad. 'You need to rest that arm, not go whacking drums with it.'

My shoulders slump and I blow out a long loud sigh.

'Hey,' Dad says, 'it's not the end of the world.'

Little does he know.

Very little, actually.

I've never told Dad about my time travelling. I've thought about it, but . . . perhaps I'm afraid he won't believe me. Because then what? Questions, and doctors, and worried looks from the teachers. Or maybe I'm afraid that he will believe me, because what then? More questions, more doctors, perhaps a few scary scientists.

I know I'll have to tell him one day, and it crosses my mind that now might be the perfect time. Actually, Dad, it really could be the end of the world. I'm a time traveller, you see, and the future's stuffed with zombies and it's down to me to fix it. Oh and by the way, in the future you live in a nice cottage by the seaside.

It would be a relief to get it all off my chest. A massive relief. I open my mouth to speak and . . .

. . . Dad fills it with a spoonful of chocolate ice-cream.

It's very good ice-cream.

And maybe it's just as well. I've got a lot to do tonight. Like coming up with a plan to win Griffin's Got Talent and save the world before one o'clock tomorrow afternoon. A task that would be a lot easier if I hadn't attempted to shift Gloria Dismal in a wheelbarrow and ended up breaking my arm.

I tap my plaster cast on the edge of the table.

'I'm such a wally!'

'Don't be so hard on yourself,' says Dad. 'What's done is done.'

'Even if what's done shouldn't have been done?'

'Even then.'

I know Dad means well, but the fact is, if I'd kept my cool and not insisted on sending Gloria home, then maybe my wrist would still be in one piece and I might have a chance of saving the world from a plague of zombies.

'Your mum was always better at this kind of thing,' Dad says.

I feel tears come to my eyes, but I've got quite good at holding them back. The trick is to sit still and not try to speak. If you try to speak, the tears find their way through.

Dad taps the tip of my nose with the cold spoon, and there will be a brown splodge there now. He smiles. 'But, I think I know what Mum would have said.'

I nod, but I don't speak.

'She'd have said, "Don't dwell on the past, Bob. Live in the moment. And there's no way you're shoving a drumstick down your cast."'

I laugh. A loud strong honk of laughter that makes a little bit of chocolate ice-cream shoot out of my nose.

'You know what, Dad?'

Dad says What? with his eyes.

'I'd say you're pretty good at this kind of thing, actually.'

Dad ruffles my hair. Then he feeds me another scoop of ice-cream, and takes one more for himself.

WALKIE-TALKIES WAY PAST BEDTIME. OVER.
GOOD EVENING MRS. SCHNITZEL. OVER.
A PLAN. OVER.
WINDING UP MICKEY. OVER.

I keep my walkie-talkie under my pillow. It's not particularly comfortable, but it means I don't have to get out of bed if I want to contact the Schnitzel or the Schnitzel wants to contact me. They have a range of three miles, which is more than enough – Malcolm only lives three doors down, and if we hung out of the windows we could have a perfectly good conversation without shouting. Much. Which is exactly what we used to do before he gave me a set of walkie-talkies for my eleventh birthday. (Strictly speaking he only gave me one walkie-talkie, as he kept the other for himself. Which is just as well, otherwise I'd have no one to talkie with.)

I press the talk button. 'Schnitzel, do you read me? Over.'

My handset crackles. 'Reading you loud and clear, Bob. How's your wrist? Over.'

'Broken. Both bones. Over.'

'Ouch. Over.'

'Tell me about it. Over.'

'Do you think you could shove a drumstick down your cast? Over.'

I sigh. 'Dad won't let me. Over.'

'So I guess our chances of winning GGT are over. Over.'

'Maybe not over. Over.'

'What do you mean, not over over? Over.'

'I mean it's not over until it's over. Over.'

I hear a noise downstairs. Dad in the kitchen probably. Well, I hope so, otherwise we're being burgled. I hold my breath and listen. A tap runs. Someone burps loudly. If it is a burglar, they're not a very good one.

'Bob? Are you there? Over.'

'Still here,' I whisper into the walkie-talkie. 'What if we beat Eno at his own game? Over.'

'But we're not inventors, Bob. We're rockers. Over.'

'Exactly. Rock music is the single greatest musical invention since cavemen made the first drum out of stretched dinosaur skin and some mammoth bones. So how hard can it be to invent something better than a selfie hat? Over.'

'Good point. Over.'

Through the walkie-talkie I hear Malcolm's bedroom door open. I know it's his door, because it has a very distinctive squeak. Someone walks into his room, and then, 'Malcolm! What have I told you about talking on that thing after lights out? It's late and you know you get grumpy if you don't get enough beddy-bobos. Now say goodnight to Robert and turn that walkie-squawkie off. Over.'

'Sorry Mum. Over.'

'Fine,' says Malcolm's mum. 'And goodnight, Robert. Over.'

'Good night, Mrs Schnitzel,' I say into the walkie-talkie. 'Over.'

The sound of a door closing and of Malcolm's mum's footsteps fading away.

'I'm back,' says Schnitz. 'Over.'

'Beddy-bobos?' I say, laughing. 'Over.'

'Shut up, Robert. So, what's the plan? Over.'

'Meet me in the garage, first thing tomorrow. We'll invent something before we leave for school. Over.'

'OK,' says Malcolm. 'I'll be there at seven thirty. Over.'

'Make it eight. An hour should be plenty of time to save the world. Over and out.'

I set my bedside clock to wake me up at 7.57 so I'll have time to brush my teeth and grab an apple before Malcolm comes over. I turn off the light and try to sleep.

But sleep doesn't come.

And not just because the future is overrun with zombies. Although that is a bit of a worry. But because I miss my mum. I miss her all the time. Sometimes that missing slips into the background for a while. Other times, it's right up front. Like at Christmas, or on her birthday, or when Dad drinks his coffee out of what used to be Mum's favourite cup. Or like tonight, listening to Malcolm's mum tell him he needs his 'beddy-bobos'.

I'd give anything to hear Mum's voice again; to hear her tell a joke or sing in the shower, to tell me I'll get grumpy if I don't get my bobos. Because I do. And I have to save the world tomorrow, which is going to be hard enough without me being all cranky.

My alarm clock ticks in the dark.

Tic tic tic tic tic . . .

I count the tics and, when I've counted to one hundred, I get out of bed, go to my drawers and remove the small plain brown box that's buried at the back under a pile of T-shirts. I slide open the box and remove the watch from inside. The strap has a crease in it where the previous owner – my mum – used to fasten it on her wrist. I put the watch on, buckling the strap along the old faded crease. It's a bit loose, but it fits well enough.

I set the time, and wind the watch.

For a moment, nothing happens.

And then the watch begins to tick. The second hand travels a full circle around the watch face and Mickey Mouse's hand moves one minute forward.

'It's about time,' I say to myself. Then I climb back into bed and immediately fall asleep.

CINNAMON BUNS.
A GANG, A TEAM, A CREW ETC.
SELF-TYING SHOELACES
AND ROBOT BEES.
CHEATING.

According to Mickey Mouse, it's one minute to eight o'clock in the morning when I open the garage door.

Malcolm isn't there. But Gloria Dismal is.

'Nice watch,' says Dismal. 'It's . . . different.'

'Thank you. And what are you doing here?'

'Ooh,' says Gloria. 'Someone's cranky.'

I don't even bother denying it.

'I'm here to help,' says Dismal. 'With this inventing thing.'

I hold up my broken arm. 'Haven't you helped enough?'

'I didn't pick up the wheelbarrow,' Gloria says, walking past me and flopping down on a bag of potting compost.

'Hang on a minute. How do you know about the inventing thing?'

'I've already told you,' says Gloria. 'Thin walls. Your bedroom's right next to mine.'

'Well, you shouldn't listen. Put your fingers in your ears or something.'

Gloria pokes her tongue out at me and reaches into her ginormous bag.

'Whatever you're about to pull out of there, Gloria, I don't want it.'

Gloria removes her hand from the bag. She is holding a cinnamon bun – a deep red cherry on top, sunk to half its depth in soft white icing. The smell is amazing.

'Your loss,' says Gloria, then she takes a bite and crosses her eyes in pleasure.

'Morning, gang.'

I spin around to see the Schnitzel rolling his bike down the driveway.

'Gang? What are you talking about? Gloria's just leaving, aren't you, Gloria?'

Gloria produces another bun, which she holds out to Malcolm. 'Cinnamon thingy?'

'Nice one, Glo,' says Malcolm, taking a massive bite. 'Nice watch, Bob. New?'

'Thanks, yeah, kind of.'

'Sure you don't want one?' Dismal says, eyeing me with a smile.

'Fine,' I say. 'But it doesn't mean we're a gang.'

'Team, then,' says Gloria. 'Squad, crew, tribe, troop, posse. Whatever makes you comfortable.' She throws the cinnamon bun to me.

I catch it with my left hand, but – because I'm right-handed – it's more of a grab than a catch and my fingers sink into the warm dough. I take a bite and the bun tastes every bit as good as it looks and smells, and for maybe two minutes the only sounds in the garage are chewing, finger licking and satisfied Hmmhmmhmm-ing.

'So,' says Gloria, 'down to business. Let's talk about inventing.'

'Ahem, Gloria. I called this meeting, this is my plan, and I'll thank you to let me take charge of it.'

Gloria shrugs. 'Suit yourself.'

'Good. Thank you. So, let's talk about inventing.'

'How about a cloud of remote-controlled snow?' says Malcolm.

I know from the way our teachers talk to us that it's important to be encouraging, so I do my most enthusiastic face at Malcolm's insane idea. 'Sounds great, Malcolm. Really great. Anything else?'

'Telepathic cat,' he says. 'Robot bees, self-tying

shoelaces, light-activated torch, flying teapot, intelligent pencil, pop-up teleporter, unmeltable ice-cream, unburstable bubble gum, clip-on wings, spare eyes, chocolate-flavoured broccoli – I call that one choccoli – spreadable hair, fast-growing acorns, a cure for the common cold, self-riding bicycles, miniature elephants, self-cleaning underpants, floating milk, trained snakes, electric spoon, adjustable grass, fish-tank toilet seat, everlasting socks, wearable pasta, see-through cows and an inflatable helicopter.'

'That it?'

Malcolm scratches his head. 'I thought maybe the robot bees could also have lasers.'

'Well done,' I say, doing my best, but struggling, to remain encouraging. 'And how would any of those, you know, work?'

Malcolm shrugs. 'I'm just the ideas guy. Thought maybe you could do the making bit.'

'It took me two days to put a bell on my handlebars

and I got a D in design technology. How am I supposed to build a helicopter?'

'What about the telepathic cat?' says Malcolm.

'Malcolm, I can't stop Zem eating my socks, let alone train a cat. Let alone a telepathic one.'

Gloria clears her throat. 'I have an idea,' she says, reaching – of course – into her bag. 'After I overheard you going on about inventing last night –'

'Overheard? It's called being nosy.'

'Anyway,' says Gloria, ignoring me, 'I scribbled out some ideas, and came up with something quite exciting.'

'Why do I suspect it involves tambourines?' I say.

'Correctamundo,' says Dismal, pulling a tambourine from her bag.

It has something that looks like a pink plastic handle taped to the side.

'Cool,' says Malcolm. 'What is it?'

'You know electric guitars?' says Gloria.

'Don't tell me,' I say. 'An electric tambourine?'

'Exactly,' says Gloria. 'Wait, have you been to the future again?'

I shake my head. 'Just a lucky guess.'

'What's the handle thingy?' Malcolm says.

'It was my electric toothbrush. But . . .'

She pushes a button on her toothbrush and it buzzes into life, sending a wave of vibrations up the handle to the tambourine, which tinkles gently.

'That's it?' I say. 'A tambourine taped to a toothbrush?'

Gloria gives the button on her toothbrush another push. 'A two-speed tambourine,' she says, and the thing goes into overdrive, the tiny cymbals rattling at high, and highly irritating, speed.

'Awesome,' says Malcolm.

'Thank you,' says Gloria. 'I thought so.'

'Listen,' I say, 'Eno Fezzinuff has invented a smile-activated selfie hat. And you think we're going to beat him to the prize with an electric tambourine?'

'Correction,' says Dismal, 'a turborine.'

'Whatever it's called, it's . . .'

Gloria looks at me, waiting for the next word to leave my mouth. She looks excited, as if she's expecting that word to be awesome, amazing, or genius. When in reality, that word was going to be ridiculous. But looking at her excited face now, I feel rotten. Even if the turborine is ridiculous.

'Yes?' says Gloria.

'It's a good idea,' I say.

She smiles.

'If you're into tambourines,' I add.

She smiles and nods.

'I'm just . . . not sure it's what we're looking for. At this particular moment.'

Gloria's smile vanishes.

'So what are we looking for?' she asks, sounding mildly miffed. 'At this particular moment?'

'Something like a smile-activated selfie hat,' I say. 'Only better.'

'Not having it stuck to your head would be an improvement,' says Gloria.

'Like if it could fly,' says Malcolm.

'Yes!' says Gloria.

'We could use robot bees?' tries Malcolm.

'No. Not bees . . .' my mind flashes back to the future with its crowded skies full of all-terrain craft and . . .

'Drones!' I say. 'We'll make a selfie drone!'

'Brilliant,' says Malcolm. 'And how exactly are we going to do that?'

My shoulders slump.

'We could . . .' Gloria looks like she's uncertain whether or not she should finish her sentence.

'What, Gloria?'

She bites her bottom lip, looks over her shoulder as if to check we're not being overheard. And then she says it: 'We could . . . cheat.'

'Did you just say cheat?'

'I wouldn't normally suggest it,' says Gloria. 'But . . .

well, this is to save the world, right?'

'Right.'

'So we cheat.'

'OK,' I say. 'Cheat how?'

'Malcolm,' says Gloria, 'you've got a little drone thingy, haven't you?'

'The D-Rex 3000,' says Malcolm.

'Excellent,' says Gloria. 'Go get it.'

Introducing the Face-Activated Flying Personal Image Capture System.

Or FAFPICS, for short.

Using Malcolm's D-Rex 3000, Malcolm's sister's karaoke microphone, Gloria's fitness-tracking step-counting Bluetooth smart watch, my dad's old mobile phone with a cracked screen, a pair of knitting needles, a torch and a great deal of black tape, we have constructed a machine that still – just about – flies. Although the FAFPICS is making some worrying noises under the weight of all the add-ons – imagine the sound of a food blender full of broken glass, robot bees and custard, and you have the general idea.

The knitting needles have been positioned so they look like a pair of futuristic antennae. The phone with the broken screen is taped on the front. And the microphone dangles from the underside on a spring taken from Gloria's joke spectacles. The torch is there to shine in the judges' eyes and stop them looking too closely, in which case they would almost certainly see what a load of rubbish this thing really is.

It works like this:

Malcolm goes on stage to present the FAFPICS.

I hide under the stage with the drone's remote control.

Gloria will be in the audience, controlling the camera on my dad's broken phone with her Bluetooth watch. Malcolm will do a bit of commanding, the drone will do a bit of flying, and – the big finale – Malcolm smiles,

Gloria presses a button on her fitness thingy, and the phone takes Malcolm's selfie. At which point, the crowd bursts into applause, the judges award us the £50 prize, Eno goes home disappointed, and the world is saved from a zombie apocalypse.

It's hard to imagine what could possibly go wrong.

THE FAFPICS.
BACK TO FRONT AND UPSIDE DOWN.
VARIOUS WORRYING NOISES.
SMOKE AND HAMSTERS.

It's dark down here. Very dark.

Above the stage, the lights are bright and Griffin's Got Talent is underway, but down here – beneath the stage – it's dark as a cave, the only light coming from small gaps in the boards above my head. There's just enough light to see the controls for the FAFPICS. And the cobwebs that hang from every surface.

I would have brought a torch, but we used it for the FAFPICS. And soon, our ridiculous invention will have its moment in the spotlight.

So far, on the stage above my head we have had:

A tap-dance by Sandra Katana from Year 12 – which, down here, was like being in a coffin while someone hammered nails into the lid. All that banging brought down a good deal of dust, too, and it took a tremendous effort not to sneeze and cough my lungs up.

Next up was Maria Mamooli, Year 8, juggling her hamsters. A much quieter act, with only the occasional soft thud as, presumably, her concentration slipped.

Jeremy Dither, Year 9, spent five minutes doing bird impersonations – whistling, basically – and from down here they all sounded pretty much the same. And not at all like any bird I've ever heard.

There has been a magician, a ventriloquist, a comedian (luckily a not very funny one, so I didn't have to worry about laughing and being discovered), a violinist, a cellist, and an oboist. Jamal Smith has just finished playing the spoons – he was surprisingly good, but he wasn't Tentacles-of-Time good.

The most annoying thing about the whole experience is this: now I've seen the competition (well, seen bits of it through the gaps in the stage) I'm more convinced than ever that if I hadn't broken my wrist, the Tentacles of Time would easily have won the whole thing.

There are only two acts left now – Malcolm and Eno. Although if all goes according to plan – and why wouldn't it? – Eno might as well go home now and take his selfie hat with him.

Above me, Mr Huffman walks across the stage and pauses in front of the microphone. 'A big round of applause for Jamal Smith, please. I think we can all agree he was . . . spoontacular!'

Mr Huffman pauses for laughter.

Doesn't get any.

Someone clears their throat.

'Right,' says Mr Huffman. 'Fine. Please put your hands together and welcome on stage Malcolm

Schnitzel and his Face-Activated Flying Personal Image Capture System.'

The audience claps, but not much.

Malcolm takes the centre of the stage. From down here I can't see much of Malcolm, just the soles of his shoes and a clear view up his nostrils. He is holding the FAFPICS in his left hand, the invention hidden beneath one of Dad's tea towels. The tea towel is decorated with kittens, but it was the cleanest one we had.

'Thank you, Mr Huffman,' says Malcolm. 'Today, I would like to present a solution to perhaps one of the biggest challenges facing humanity. How to take a selfie . . .' dramatic pause '. . . without using . . .' another dramatic pause '. . . your hands!!!'

When we rehearsed this speech earlier, we imagined there'd be a tremendous cheer at this point.

There is no cheer. Tremendous or otherwise.

'Right,' says Malcolm. He clears his throat. 'Fellow students of Griffin High, behold the . . . FAFPICS!'

He whips the tea towel off the drone.

No one gasps, claps or shows any sign of being impressed.

'Rise!' says Malcolm.

Beneath the stage, I turn the remote control on. I push a small lever forward.

On stage, I hear the motor of the FAFPICS whir into life, hear the propellers spin, hear the amazed gasp of the audience as the FAFPICS lifts from Malcolm's outstretched hand. Hear the rather worrying sound of robot bees in a blender.

'Left,' says Malcolm.

And I push the lever left.

And something I didn't expect – the sound of laughter from the audience.

'I said, left!' says the Schnitzel.

So I push left again.

More laughter.

Malcolm stamps on the floorboards, making them

squeak and sending down a shower of dust and cobwebs. I blink the dust out of my eyes and squint upwards through the gaps between the boards. And now I see my mistake – Schnitzel is facing the audience, while I am facing the Schnitzel. His left is my right; his right is my left.

I flip the controller around, push the switch to the left and the FAFPICS swings around in the desired direction.

The audience claps. It's actually working!

'And now,' says the Schnitz, 'for a selfie.'

Through the boards, I see Dad's camera phone flash.

The audience cheers. Actually cheers.

And somewhere in the darkness and dust beneath the stage . . . something squeaks. I hear the sound of scurrying feet – a mouse, perhaps, or a rat. My skin crawls, and I need Malcolm to land the FAFPICS and get off stage before something horrible runs up my leg.

'Down,' says Malcolm.

I push the switch down on the remote control, but as I watch, the FAFPICS rises higher into the air.

The audience laughs.

The creature beneath the stage squeaks.

'Down!' says Malcolm.

I stare at the remote controller and realise my mistake – when I flipped it around to swap left and right, I also swapped up and down. Quickly, I push the small lever in the opposite direction.

But the FAFPICS does not respond. It continues to hover above the stage. The noise it's making is painful, and I can smell burning. Which can't be good.

'Down!' says Malcolm.

The scurrying thing beneath the stage squeaks.

And . . . wouldn't you just believe it . . . I get the tingles.

They're mild at this point – a gentle tickling on the ankles – but they are travelling steadily up my leg (just the left one, which is unusual) and it won't be long before I get the drags and lurch twenty years into the future. A future, hopefully, without zombies.

If only I can hold out long enough for Malcolm to finish the act and win GGT.

But our chances are not looking good. Our chances are – literally – going up in smoke.

The FAFPICS begins to spin, and a trail of grey smoke and sparks is pouring out from the back end. It looks like some sort of remote-controlled tornado. Which, now that I think of it, would have been a pretty good invention.

'Stop!' shouts Malcolm.

I push and pull all the levers, trying to get the drone to do something, anything, but it continues to rise and spin and smoke.

The tingles are travelling up my back and across my shoulders and neck with a sensation like tiny scrabbling claws.

'Please stop!' says Malcolm to the out-of-control FAFPICS.

The audience aren't laughing now. They gasp and shout and panic. I turn the controller to the FAFPICS off, but nothing happens. I open the back and pull the batteries free, but again, nothing happens. Someone screams. Someone always screams.

I feel the tingles on my cheek now. And this – like feeling them in just one leg – is very unusual. Something squeaks. Something close to my ear and extremely fluffy.

I turn my head, slowly, and find myself face to face with a fat brown hamster.

Above me, the FAFPICS bursts into flames and plummets towards the stage. It thuds onto the boards with a loud bang, sending a shower of sparks onto me and what must be one of Maria Mamooli's hamsters.

There is a smell of singed hair and fur.

And now I get the tingles. The real ones this time.

Not a juggled hamster scrabbling up my trouser leg.

I get the drags.

And I'm gone.

14

A FRETFUL PLAYGROUND.
THE HUMAN HOSEPIPE.
THE DIFFERENCE BETWEEN CHILDISH
AND CHILDLIKE.
DOOMED AGAIN.

It's still dark and there is a spooky creaking noise in the distance. I'm in the fort at the top of the slide. Again.

'Hey Bob,' says Future Me.

'You!' I say, and I punch my future self hard on the shoulder.

'Ow! What the heck was that for?'

'You shoved me down a slide into the clutches of a zombie. That's what.'

Future Me laughs. 'Oh that. Sorry, I forgot, it's been nearly twenty years.'

'Not for me, it hasn't.' And I go to punch him again, but Future Me sees it coming and catches me by the wrist. He stares at my hand, clutched in his. At the Mickey Mouse watches we are both wearing.

'Nice watch,' he says, releasing my hand. 'Suits you.'

'Don't change the subject. Did it occur to you that you nearly got me turned into a zombie? That could have sent the whole apocalypse back in time?'

'Well obviously not or I wouldn't have done it. Probably. But it's a good point, we should be more careful.'

'We?'

'We're the same person, Bob.'

'You might be,' I say. 'But I'm not.'

'That doesn't make any sense.'

'It makes perf—'

A voice interrupts me. It sounds like a lady, but

there's something not quite real about it – like those smart speakers some people have at home. The ones that tell you the time, or the weather, or play music. Malcolm has one that pretends it doesn't understand him when he asks it to say rude words.

'Injury detected,' says the voice. 'You have a' – there is a pause – 'fracture of the right ulna and radius bones. Please use the slide with extreme caution. And perhaps avoid the monkey bars. Thank you.'

I look around the fort for the source of this voice but see no one except Future Me. 'What was that?'

'Intelligent playgrounds,' he says with a sigh. 'Health and safety nonsense.'

'Why wasn't it like this last time we were here?'

Future Me shrugs. 'The future is a delicate thing. Who knows what past event set this particular nonsense in motion? Maybe a butterfly landed on a roundabout and somehow affected the future.'

'That doesn't sound very likely.'

'Or maybe it happened after you set Malcolm on fire.'

'No! Did he . . . is he . . . is he OK?'

'He's fine,' says Future Me. 'A spark landed on his shorts, but the moment they caught fire, he wet himself and put it out. People started calling him the human hosepipe after that.'

'Oh, thank goodness. I don't suppose we won the vouchers?'

Future Me shakes his head. 'You suppose correctly. The only thing we won was four weeks of detention.'

'And the world is still overrun with selfie zombies?'

'See for yourself,' he says, nodding to the night outside the fort. 'And be very quiet.'

Slowly, I poke my head through the opening at the top of the slide. And there they are, just beyond the playground gate – three clusters of brainless, aimless zombies, shuffling in their slow-moving huddles and grinning for selfies. They look almost harmless from here, but I've seen close up what they're capable of and I'm not keen on a repeat performance.

'Do they know you're here?' I ask.

'No,' says Future Me. 'Not yet.'

'Hang on, if the world is still overrun with zombies, what are you doing out here?'

'Malcolm dropped the banana bread again.'

'What happened this time?'

Future Me laughs. 'I shot an elastic band at his bum while he was taking the loaf out of the oven.'

'Don't you think that was a bit . . . childish?'

'No,' says Future Me, holding up a finger for emphasis. 'I do not. Childlike, yes. Childish, no. There's a big difference – allow me to explain.'

'Do I have a choice?'

Future Me doesn't bother acknowledging my question. Which is just another way of saying, No, Bob, you don't.

'Childish,' he says, 'is being sulky or spoiled or

throwing a tantrum when things don't go your way. Childlike is taking joy in simple things, having fun, being daft, being carefree.'

'Example,' I say.

'Oh, I dunno, like playing on the swings, playing with your food, pulling silly faces in the mirror, dancing in public, rolling down hills, farting when someone pulls your finger.'

'And shooting elastic bands at your best friend's bum?'

'Exactly,' says Future Me. 'These things are important.'

'Fine,' I say. 'Fair enough. But after Malcolm dropped the cake, didn't it occur to you to maybe not go to the shops this time? That you might possibly get attacked by zombies?'

'Love makes you do crazy things,' says Future Me.

I shudder. 'I really wish you wouldn't use that word.'

'What word?' says Future Me. 'Love?'

'Stop it,' I say, holding my hands over my ears.

'L-O-V-E,' says Future Me, spelling it out. And then, 'L-O-R-I.'

L-O-R-I?

I say the word out loud. 'Lori? What's a Lori?'

Future Me holds his hand to his mouth as if he's said something he shouldn't have and is trying somehow to cram the escaped word back behind his lips. 'Nothing,' he says, from behind his hand. 'Slip of the tongue.'

'Wait, is that . . . is that her name? Lori?'

'Some things it's best you don't know,' says Future Me. 'Ripples in time and all that.' And he mimes zipping his mouth, locking it and throwing away the key.

'Well, how about you tell me what you're doing up this slide. Again.'

Future Me mimes finding a key, unlocking and then unzipping his mouth. 'Well, Malcolm dropped the cake, so we got on our bikes and headed out to get more, very expensive, bananas. We got to the park, saw the zombies and took cover here.'

I hold up my hand as if I were in a classroom.

'Yes, Bob?'

'Where is Malcolm? They didn't get him, did they? The zombies?'

'Nooooo. We're not daft. He's down there.' And he flicks his eyes out across the playground.

'Don't tell me. He's on the roundabout, isn't he?'

Future Me nods. 'That man loves a roundabout.'

I poke my head outside of the fort and see Schnitzel – the great big fool – lying flat on the platform, one foot dangling over the edge and pushing the roundabout in slow circles. It's nice to see him restored to normal. Even if normal is a grown man playing on a roundabout.

'You're sure you two are thirty-one?' I whisper. 'Not, you know, three?'

'Hey, there's nothing to say you have to stop enjoying playground apparatus just because you can grow a beard. That's ageist.'

'And that,' I say, pointing towards my tattooed, blue-haired best friend playing on a roundabout, 'is just odd. It's not even a good hiding place.'

But as I say it, one of the zombie clusters begins to shuffle away from the playground, perhaps drawn by some movement or sound; perhaps because they are simply bored. And then the other two clusters follow.

'Ahem,' says Future Me. 'Turns out you don't know everything, after all. Right, let's get the Schnitz and get out of here.'

Future Me cups his hands to his mouth and calls to Malcolm in a loud whisper. 'Schnitz.'

But the Schnitz – lost in his thoughts as the roundabout turns in lazy circles – doesn't hear.

'Schnitzel!' I try in a slightly louder whisper.

Malcolm looks up.

Sees me.

And screams.

'Where did he come from?' he shouts to Future Me.

'He's a younger version of myself,' shouts my future self. 'Travelled from the past via some anomaly in the fabric of time.'

'Isn't that impossible?'

'Apparently not,' says my future self. 'I'll explain later.'

'Fair enough,' says the Schnitz.

'That was easy,' I say.

'Yeah,' says Future Me, 'he seems to be getting the hang of it.'

'How?'

'Every time you travel, you create a new timeline, a new possibility. And – I'm not really sure – you know the way a guitar string hums for a while after you pluck it? I think timelines do that too.'

'Like echoes?'

'That's a good way of putting it, yes. So even though Malcolm has never seen you materialise in this timeline, maybe he somehow feels the echoes of it.'

Just when I'm beginning to think our situation is improving . . .

. . . a voice on the wind says, 'Smiiile.'

And then many more voices answer, 'Smiiiiiiiiiiiiiiile.'

'Ah,' says Future Me. 'Looks like we're doomed. Again.'

THE DANGERS OF MESSING ABOUT WITH THE PAST. A ZOMBIE BUTCHER. A ZOMBIE GRANNY. BASICALLY, LOADS OF ZOMBIES.

The zombies are now advancing towards the playground.

'You'd better not be thinking of throwing me to that lot again,' I say.

'Won't need to,' says Future Me. 'They've had an upgrade since you were last here.'

'They look the same to –'

But before I can finish my sentence, something happens to the zombies' selfie hats. Tiny propellers pop out from the sides and start spinning at great speed. And one by one, the selfie hats lift into the air.

'What's happening?'

'Selfie drones,' says Future Me.

'This,' I say, 'cannot be good.'

'You have quite the gift for understatement,' says my future self unhelpfully.

The drones are all airborne now, and they have fanned out, forming a ring around the playground.

'Selfie drones,' I say under my breath. 'That was my idea.'

'Yep,' says Future Me. 'And now Eno's made it a reality. That's the danger of messing about with the past. You never know what it'll do to the future.'

'At least the gate's closed,' I say.

'Hmmm,' says Future Me. But it's not a good Hmmm. It's more of an I-wouldn't-get-too-excited-about-that Hmmm.

And now I see why. Freed from their selfie hats, the

shuffling, slow-moving zombies are no longer shuffling and no longer slow moving. They scuttle, they scurry, they scamper.

One of the zombies climbs over the playground gate, another jumps clean over it. One – an elderly looking lady zombie carrying a cat in a basket – unlatches the gate and walks through. She is followed by many more, all of them moving quickly, all of them heading for us. And above it all the air is filled with the sound of whining, whirring drones.

'Are they still . . . bitey?' I ask.

'Very much so,' says Future Me. 'And their bites are still infectious. We need to move now. You go to the swings. I'll create some sort of distraction.'

'I would not advise playing on the swings,' says the cautious electronic voice. 'Not with your broken wrist.'

'Shut up!' shout me and my future self.

And with that, Future Bob launches himself down the slide. He hits the ground running, dodges past the wobbly giraffe, ducks under the climbing nets, jinks towards the seesaw then comes face to face with a selfie zombie who looks like he was – in his pre-zombie days – a busy and somewhat careless butcher: he's heavy around the middle, wearing a thoroughly blood-stained apron and clutching an enormous meat cleaver.

'Smiilllllle,' says the zombie butcher, lunging at my future self.

Future Me doesn't smile. Future Me screams.

He zigs past the zombie and straight into the path of the granny zombie. 'Ssssmmiiiiiiiiillllle,' she says and her false teeth drop from her mouth. The cat in her basket hisses, and I see that it too has become zombified.

Trapped between the two, Bob does the only thing he can – he climbs up onto the seesaw. Standing at the centre of the beam, he rocks his weight one way then the other, making the seesaw pitch up and down as if it's being ridden by a pair of invisible children.

'Please do not stand on the seesaw,' says the playground, which may be intelligent but is also a real spoilsport.

'Too late for that now,' says Future Me, and he lets out a wild bark of laughter that echoes across the playground. 'Now, Bob!' he shouts. 'Go now!'

'Maximum roundabout speed exceeded,' says the playground. 'Reduce speed now.'

I glance towards Malcolm who has the roundabout spinning frighteningly fast. He is surrounded by a swarm of selfie drones and swinging at them with his smart bat.

'Defence protocols initiated,' says a robotic voice in the air above us, and a shower of bright orange sparks shoot from the underside of the drones. And I suppose that, too, was inspired by the out-of-control FAFPICS.

'Bob!' shouts my future self. 'Move it!'

I throw myself down the slide, lying flat and belly up, which really is the only way to ride a slide.

The voice of the playground sighs. 'I give up,' it says. 'Honestly, I just give up.'

As I hit the end of the slide, I jump up and set off running towards the swings. There's no reason to walk across the balance beam, but I do it anyway, because I'm in that kind of mood.

'What now?' I shout.

'Swing!' shouts Future Me from his seesaw.

'Well obviously!' I shout back.

'Get enough momentum and you might just clear the fence,' he says.

'That's crazy!'

'I know,' shouts my future self. 'But it's that or the zombies. Your choice!'

'He does make a logical point,' says the futuristic playground.

So I do the only thing I can – I start swinging.

The night air is cool on my face as I swing in higher and higher arcs, my legs kicking out in front and the seat rising way above the height of the fence. I'd forgotten how much fun the swings are, and my future self was right – I really should get to the playground more often.

'Go Bob go!' shouts Malcolm.

Malcolm swings his bat and thwacks one of the selfie drones. It spirals out of control, trailing a long streamer of sparks as it zips through the night and crashes into the sandpit. The Schnitz seems to have found his aim now and he connects with two more drones, sending them flying and lighting up the sky like an out-of-control firework display.

Future Me is having less luck. The zombies – even without their selfie hats – continue to swarm around him. My future self kicks the seesaw up and down in big thumping movements. He's breathing heavily, and the zombie hoard is three deep at his feet.

'It's now or never,' he shouts in my direction. 'Jump!'

'I've got a broken arm!'

'Then land on your feet!' says my future self, laughing at his own joke.

And the intelligent playground laughs too. I'm not sure if it's possible for artificial intelligence units to lose their mind, but when this one laughs the sound makes my ears itch.

'Jump, Bob, jump!' cackles the voice of the playground.

'Then what?'

'Go back and save the world!' shouts Future Me.

'What about you and Malcolm?'

'We'll be fine,' shouts Future Me.

'Will we?' shouts Future Malcolm, who is looking unsteady on his feet from all the spinning.

'I wouldn't bet on it!' shouts the once-intelligent playground with a hoot of laughter.

The zombie butcher chooses this moment to make a grab for Future Me's leg. Future Me kicks out at the butcher, but in doing so, loses his balance and falls backwards into the hands of several waiting zombies.

'Warned you!' says the voice of the playground. 'But you wouldn't listen! Hahahahahaha!'

'See you in the next future!!!' shouts Future Me, and he vanishes beneath the zombies, screaming like a baby.

The moon is bright tonight and the scene is lit in a spooky white glow as the zombies claw at my future body. Without their selfie hats and cameras, the monsters are no longer interested in posing for pictures – they are entirely focused on attack. Like spiders with a fly, cats with a mouse or . . . well, like a pack of zombies with a hunk of warm meat.

'Get your filthy hands off my best friend!' shouts Malcolm, waving his smart bat in the air. It's one brief moment of lost concentration, but one moment is all the selfie drones need.

They close in on Malcolm, their cameras flash, and Malcolm releases his grip on the roundabout railing. He hits the ground with a thud. And while his body is motionless, his hair flickers through all the colours of the rainbow. For one entire second the night is still and quiet, and then Malcolm climbs to his feet, his tattoos buzzing and bright and spelling out a single word across every inch of his skin: smile!

Malcolm points at me and shouts the call of the zombies: 'Ssssmmiiiiiiiilllle.'

I tuck my legs beneath me then kick them out hard in front as the swing curves and rises upwards. And at the top of the swing, I release my grip on the chains and sail free and clear into the inky black night.

The wind whips at my hair.

I get the tingles.

I get the drags.

You know the rest.

DOING THE DAY ALL OVER AGAIN.
SMASHING STUFF UP.
BUT FOR A GOOD REASON.
PLAN B.

I'm back in the past, standing in the cool, quiet and dusty space of Dad's garage. My heart is beating hard, my forehead is damp with sweat and my eyes are still watering from my death-defying swing through the cold night air.

But here – now – all is still.

No drones, no zombies, no screaming.

Sunlight shines through the gap at the bottom of the closed garage door. From outside come the sounds of birds tweeting, a dog barking, and the utter silence of Gloria Dismal, who is waiting on the other side of the door. In about thirty seconds, Malcolm will join her and we will do the day all over again.

I pause for a moment and breathe deeply, enjoying this brief moment of calm before everything – once again – goes full-on bonkers.

Five – four – three – two – and here we go again . . .

'Morning Glo,' says Malcolm's voice from outside. 'What you doing here?'

I raise the garage door. 'She's here to help, aren't you Gloria?'

Gloria looks at me suspiciously.

Malcolm does the same. 'You invited Gloria?'

I shake my head. 'Thin walls. Isn't that right, Gloria.'

'You're weird,' says Gloria as she walks into the garage and flops down on a bag of potting compost.

'And she's brought cinnamon buns,' I add.

'Very weird,' she says, producing a brown paper bag of pastries.

My stomach rumbles.

'Charming,' says Gloria, handing me a pastry then passing one to Malcolm.

The pastry is warm, the icing is sweet, and I gobble the lot in three big bites.

'Thank you,' I say, wiping flakes of pastry from my chin. 'I needed that.'

'Didn't you eat breakfast?' Gloria asks.

I nod. 'Yeah, but it was a very long time ago.'

'Tell me about it,' says Gloria, thrusting a hand into the unknowable depths of her bag. 'I've been up since six working on my –'

'Turborine?' I say, which earns me yet another funny look.

Gloria pulls the instrument from her bag. 'You time travelled?'

I nod. 'Just got back.'

'Awesome!' says Gloria, who seems to have no problem believing the frankly crazy idea that I can pass through time as easily as other people pass from one room to another.

'Not so awesome actually,' I say. 'The inventing thing didn't work. In fact, it just made things a whole lot worse.'

Gloria looks at her tamborine with disappointment.

'It's not your fault,' I tell her. 'The whole idea of us trying to beat Eno at his own game was a bad one.'

'What about the robot bees?' says Malcolm. 'The choccoli? The self-tying shoelaces?'

'I'm sure they would have been great,' I say. 'And the turborine. The problem is time. We just don't have enough of it.'

'So what do we do now?'

'We need to come up with a plan that doesn't involve trying to out-invent an inventor.'

'We could set a swarm of robot bees on him,' says Malcolm.

'Robot bees don't exist, Malcolm. Remember?'

'Right,' he says. 'Sorry.'

'We could kidnap him,' Gloria says. 'Kidnap Eno.'

Malcolm and I turn slowly towards Gloria.

'Are you crazy?' I say. Which is a waste of a question because I already know the answer.

'What?' she says innocently. 'What's wrong?'

'Kidnapping, Gloria, is a serious crime. Usually one that involves bashing people over the head, tying them up and throwing them in the back of a van.'

Gloria takes a moment to consider this. 'So you're saying we need to get some rope and a van?'

'No, Gloria, I'm saying we are not kidnapping Eno because kidnapping is a very bad and very illegal thing to do.'

Gloria sighs as if I'm being a complete party-pooper. 'Fine,' she says. 'What's your suggestion for saving the world?'

'Why don't we just . . .' Malcolm shrugs, 'smash it up?'

I turn my attention from Gloria to Malcolm.

'Smash what up?'

'His invention, of course. If it's as dangerous as you say it is, then we have to. For humanity an' whatnot.'

'OK,' I say. 'We smash it up. But let's call it sabotage.'

'Sure,' says Malcolm. 'What's sabotage?'

'Smashing stuff up,' I say. 'But for a good reason.'

'No better reason that saving civilisation as we know it,' says Gloria.

And this is Plan B.

GLORIA STEPS UP.
HORRIBLE THINGS IN JARS.
NO NO NO NO NO NO NO!
MY MIDDLE NAME IS JOYCE.

Not so long ago, I was beneath the school stage, covered in dust and cobwebs. This time, I'm on the stage itself, behind the curtain, peeping through a small gap at the waiting audience.

The school hall is packed with everyone not performing in the talent show, which is everyone in the school minus about twenty people. They are squashed together on plastic chairs, benches and the floor. This isn't like those TV talent shows where the audience is excited to be there. Peeping through a gap in the curtain at all the fidgeting children and bored teachers, it's obvious that most people would rather be somewhere else – anywhere else – than here.

And I feel the same way.

Sometimes you have to do a horrible thing for a good reason.

Like putting broccoli in a chicken pie because broccoli is supposed to be good for you.

Or telling your dad his moustache looks ridiculous, because his moustache looks ridiculous. Or . . . or like a doctor chopping someone's leg off to save their life.

The idea of smashing up Eno's invention does not make me feel good. I know it's an evil invention, but Eno doesn't know that – as far as he's concerned it's something he's worked extremely hard on and is extremely proud of.

I feel a little bit bad for him.

Even if he does grow up to be an evil genius.

*

While the rest of Griffin High School are squashed into the main hall and wishing they weren't, the rest of us – the acts – are shoved into Mr Huffman's windowless physics lab, waiting to be called on stage. And also wishing we weren't.

All eyes turn to me as I walk into the room.

'Are they ready for us yet?' asks Jeremy Dither.

His face is pale and sweaty. He looks like a Roman gladiator – one with no sword, shield or combat training – who is about to face a pack of hungry lions. And maybe a couple of armoured elephants for good measure.

'Not quite,' I tell him. 'Mr Huffman is making a speech about the Eight Great Griffin Values. He's only got as far as 'Not Complaining About School Dinners', so there's another five to go.'

This information does nothing to calm Jeremy's nerves.

The physics lab is small and windowless, which

only adds to the feeling that we're all awaiting some terrible fate. You can see it on the faces of the acts; the way they fidget in their chairs, the way they chew their nails, the way they stare at the floor as if looking for a way to escape. You can see it in the way Maria Mamooli's hamsters squeak and chitter. You can see it in the way Jeremy Dither just vomited in a wastepaper basket.

Everyone is nervous.

Everyone except Eno.

'You should all go home now,' he says, striding around the classroom as if he's a king and we are his subjects. Wearing his selfie hat as if it's a crown, rather than a dangerous and ludicrous invention. He also has an annoying and disgusting habit of cracking his knuckles while he strides. He does them one at a time, grabbing a single finger and giving it a quick twisting tug. Krakk!

'It's a foregone conclusion that I'm going to win,' says

Eno to the room. 'You know, I wouldn't be surprised if the judges award me second and third places as well.'

He turns to the camera dangling in front of his face, poses for yet another picture and smiles.

Snap! goes the camera phone.

Krakk!! goes Eno's left index finger.

Malcolm winces at the sound. 'I'd like to crack him,' he says under his breath.

'I'd hoped for some stronger competition,' says Eno. 'But I suppose I'll have to be content with beating a hamster juggler, a bird whistler, and a band with a one-armed drummer.'

At my side, Malcolm clenches his fists.

'Easy, Schnitzel,' I whisper. 'We'll have the last laugh.'

'When?' he says through gritted teeth. 'He hasn't taken the flipping thing off his head once.'

'Anyone care for a photograph with this year's winner?' Eno says to the room.

No one says anything.

'Surely someone wants to stand next to greatness,' says Fezzinuff. 'Who knows, perhaps a little will rub off on you.'

Gloria gets to her feet.

'I will,' she says in an admiring voice. 'I'd absolutely love to.'

Eno is as surprised as everyone else.

'What are you even doing in here?' he says. 'You're not one of the acts.'

'I'm with the band,' says Gloria.

Eno hesitates. With Gloria striding confidently towards him, he seems a little less sure of himself. It's kind of impressive.

Gloria stands next to Eno and drapes one arm around his shoulders.

Another thing about Gloria: she's the tallest person in our year by a good way. The reason for this is that Gloria Dismal is mostly made of legs. Other people are about half legs – they start at your ankles and finish in the middle of your body. Gloria is about three quarters legs. It's like someone took an eleven-year-old girl's body and sewed it to the legs of an eighteen-year-old high-jump champion. It looks like she's on stilts.

Gloria Dismal towers above everyone in our year and most people in the year above. And now, standing as straight and tall as possible, she absolutely skyscrapers over Eno.

Even standing on tiptoes and tilting his head upwards, he can't get all of him and all of Gloria into the picture. 'You're too tall,' he says.

'I think you'll find,' says Gloria, 'that your stick is too dangly.'

'I've never had this problem before,' splutters Eno.

'Let me put it on,' says Gloria. 'See if it really works.'

'Of course it works,' snaps Eno.

Gloria looks at him like she's not convinced. 'Prove it.'

Eno thinks about this for a second then slowly

removes his selfie hat. 'Be careful,' he says, handing the contraption to Gloria.

'Oh, I will,' she says, lowering the thing onto her head. 'What do I do now?'

'You smile,' says Eno, not smiling. 'That's why it's called a smile-activated selfie hat.'

Gloria stares into the camera, but she doesn't smile. She scowls. 'No,' she says, 'this won't do. This won't do at all.'

Eno is getting irritated. 'What are you on about?'

'I'm all in shadow,' says Gloria. 'I photograph best in bright sunlight, it brings out the colour of my eyes.'

And with her arm around Eno's shoulders, she strides across the classroom towards the door.

'What are you playing at?' Eno squeals.

'We'll take our picture in Mrs Gren's room across the corridor,' says Gloria. 'It's got a whole wall of windows.'

Eno's legs scrabble at the floor as he is dragged along behind Gloria, like a toddler trying to keep up with his mother. 'Put me down, you enormous fool!'

It is, and not for the first time today, quite an impressive performance by the Dismal One.

Me and Malcolm follow them across the corridor and into Mrs Gren the biology teacher's classroom. The room is like a museum – and every available space is occupied with some kind of biological exhibit: plants, fossils, a termite colony in a glass tank, gerbils in a cage. A skeleton dangles from a hook on the wall, a model showing the inside of a human body sits on a bench, and in jars around the room are the pickled floating brains of a variety of small animals. As Gloria said, the classroom is flooded with bright afternoon sunlight, which glints off the jars and their revolting contents.

'Perfect,' says Gloria, stopping in front of a large, open window.

'Nothing about this is perfect,' says Eno.

'How high are we up here?' says Gloria, poking her head out of the window.

'Four floors up!' says Eno. 'Approximately eight metres, or twenty-six point two feet. So kindly get your ridiculous head back inside.'

'Extreme selfie!' shouts Gloria, and she smiles for the camera. 'What a fun little toy.'

'Toy?' says Eno. 'Toy? There's more intelligence in that hat than there is in your hollow head and the heads of all your friends put together.'

'Hollow?' says Gloria, giving her head a shake. 'It doesn't feel hollow.'

As she shakes her head, the phone swings left and right like the pendulum on an overwound grandfather clock.

'Careful!' shouts Eno.

'Careful's my middle name,' says Gloria, nodding her head and making the phone bounce up and down like a fish struggling on a line.

And then, of course, the hat slips from Gloria's head.

Eno yelps. Actually yelps.

'No,' he says. 'No no no no no no.'

And on the seventh no, the selfie hat hits the concrete below the window.

'Oh,' says Gloria, pulling her head in from the window, 'I forgot. My middle name's Joyce, not 'Careful'. Still, what do you expect from me and my hollow head?'

Eno's expression changes from shock to anger. 'You . . . you . . . you did that on purpose.'

'Why on earth would I do that?'

'Because you knew I was going to win. And because you're a giant lunatic.'

'No need to name call,' says Gloria.

'I'm telling,' says Eno. 'I'm telling Mr Huffman. And then I'm getting my spare selfie hat and I'm still going to win.'

'Spare selfie hat?' say Gloria, Malcolm and myself at exactly the same time. And then – because the future of the world is at stake – we all say it again. 'Spare selfie hat!!'

'Of course I have a spare hat,' says Eno, setting off towards the door. 'A genius anticipates and prepares for every eventuality.'

We stare at him in disbelief.

'Oh, your faces,' says Eno smugly. 'I must remember this, it'll make an interesting chapter in my autobiography.'

'You're writing your autobiography already?' says Malcolm.

'Of course,' says Eno. 'I have a duty to history. And I already have a title.'

'Enough is Not Fezzinuff,' I say, not realising my slip until the words have escaped my mouth.

Eno stares at me very carefully, and all of a sudden I feel like a bug under a microscope. 'How could you know that?' he says.

I shrug. 'Lucky guess.'

'You're not that clever.'

'Tell him,' says Gloria.

I shush her with my eyes. And then, because this is Gloria, I use my voice too: 'Shhh!'

'Tell me what?' says Eno.

'Maybe she's right,' says Malcolm. 'Maybe if we explain, maybe that's how we save the future.'

'The future?' says Eno.

And talking of the future, here come the tingles.

'In the future, your invention turns people into mindless selfie zombies,' Gloria blurts.

'Gloria! Don't say anything else,' I say. 'It might have . . . consequences.'

Eno frowns at me and his thick black eyebrows creep towards each other. 'What do you mean, consequences?'

'Nothing,' I say. 'We've said too much already.'

'Ripples in time,' says Malcolm.

'Malcolm!' I shout. 'We've said – too – much – already.'

Eno's brow furrows. 'You actually believe this gobbledygook, don't you?'

'Totally,' says Gloria. 'Bob's a time traveller. We have proof.'

I throw up my hands in frustration. 'What part of "we've said too much already" do you two not understand?'

'Sorry,' says Malcolm.

'Oopsy,' says Gloria.

'Time traveller?' says Eno Fezzinuff.

'Don't listen to them,' I say. 'It's a . . . a silly game they like to play.'

'I don't believe you, Trebor. Something's going on here and I want to know what it is.' He grabs a finger, twists, pulls. Kkrakk.

'Must you do that?' says Malcolm. 'It's gross.'

And talking of gross, here come the drags. My vision blurs, the plastic skeleton grins at me, the jars of animal brains sparkle and flicker.

'Nothing's going on,' I say weakly.

'Time travel,' whispers the boy that will one day

become an evil genius, his voice like a whisper of bad news blown on a cold wind. 'Interesting.'

And I'm gone.

18

EMBARRASSING FRECKLES.
ALL SCREAMED OUT.
THE ISSUE WITH EVIL GENIUSES.
A TELLTALE CUCKOO.

I could be anywhere.

But I have a feeling it's nowhere good.

It's as dark as the inside of a cave and if there's another Bob nearby I can't see him. I have a strong urge to call out his name, but for all I know I'm surrounded by zombies. For all I know, Future Me is a zombie. Things didn't look too good last time I laid eyes on him. So I stand still, I breathe as quietly as possible, and I listen. And then . . .

'Bob?'

An adult voice. Familiar, but at the same time not familiar.

It echoes off the walls. Almost as if we were in a cave. But there are other sounds too. Sounds that you don't tend to hear in caves – a faint buzz of electricity. Something – cogs, maybe – turning. Ticking. Lots of ticking.

'Bob,' says the voice. 'Is that you?'

'Maybe,' I say. 'Who's asking?'

The voice chuckles. It's an odd chuckle. Slightly . . . off. Not quite right. It's a give-you-goosebumps kind of chuckle. And it does exactly that.

'It's Bob,' says the cold voice. 'Future Bob.'

'How do I know?'

'Because I know you bite your fingernails in the middle of the night and hide them inside your pillow case,' says the voice.

'Doesn't everyone?' I ask.

'OK,' says the voice claiming to be me. 'You're in a

band called the Tentacles of Time, your best friend is Malcolm Schnitzel, and you have three freckles on your left bum cheek that look like a surprised emoji.'

I think I hear laughter, but it's hard to be sure.

'Fair enough,' I say into the dark. 'You're me.'

'Exactly,' says the voice. 'And I used to be you.'

'You sound different,' I tell him.

'I suppose I am,' he says. And again, the dreadful chuckle.

'What year is this?'

'Still 2043,' says Future Me.

'Where are we?' And I have a strong feeling that I won't like the answer.

'Cave,' says the voice.

I knew it!

'Are we hiding from zombies?'

'There are no zombies in this future,' says another voice. Also familiar. Also not.

'Malcolm?'

'The one and only,' says the voice.

'You didn't scream this time,' I say.

'All screamed out,' says the voice.

And that doesn't sound good.

'But you did say there are no zombies, right?'

'That's right,' says Future Me. 'No zombies. Zero zeds.'

'So the plan worked?'

'Not exactly. We still have something of an Eno problem.'

'What sort of problem?'

I wait for one of the two voices to answer but the only response is a long and unsettling quiet. Although that word – 'unsettling' – suggests I was at some point settled. And I have not for one second since arriving here felt settled. Either way – I don't like this silence.

'What sort of problem?' I try again.

'Tell him,' says a third voice. And this one is a lady.

'How many of you are there?'

'Just the three of us,' says the lady.

'Bob,' says Future Me, 'meet Lori. Your girlfriend.'

'Hello,' I say. 'It's . . . nice to meet you.'

'Well, hello,' says Lori. 'Ah, you were so cute.'

'I still am,' says Future Me, and Lori laughs.

'So I don't know you?' I say. 'In my own time.'

There is a beat of silence, then Lori answers. 'No,' she says. 'It's a few years before you get to know me. But it's worth the wait, I promise.'

'Are you blushing?' says Future Me. 'You sound like you're blushing.'

'Of course not,' I say to the darkness. 'And anyway, how can anyone sound like they're blushing?'

'Dunno,' says Bob. 'But you do.'

'Stop teasing him,' says Lori. 'It's not so long ago you were that awkward little boy.'

Bob and Lori laugh, and the sound sends shivers up my spine.

'So,' I say. 'This cave business. What are we doing

here and can we leave? It's giving me the heebie-jeebies.'

'Not that easy,' says Future Me. 'We're sort of . . . incapacitated.'

'Captured,' says Malcolm.

'By Eno,' says Lori.

'He's . . .' Future Me trails off.

'What?' I say. 'He's what?'

'Experimenting,' says Future Me. 'He's experimenting on me.'

And in the silence that follows, I listen again to the sounds of some unseen gizmo or gadget. Buzzing sounds, clicking sounds, grinding sounds. Sounds that don't go well with the word experiment.

'What kind of experiments?' I ask nervously. 'Painless experiments? Gentle experiments? Jolly good fun experiments that everybody has a jolly good laugh about?'

'Not exactly,' says Future Me. 'No.'

'But why experiment at all?'

'Because someone told him we're a time traveller.'

Someone, somewhere in the darkness, clears their throat.

The dark feels as if it is full of horrors and I wonder if goosebumps can get goosebumps. Because if they can, then mine have.

'I wish there was some light in here,' I say.

And then there is light.

A lot of light.

Overhead, a row of fluorescent tubes flicker into life. The light is dim and tinted blue – if anything the space feels more spooky than it did in total darkness.

'What just happened?' I say.

'Voice-activated lights,' says Future Me.

'I thought you said this was a cave.'

'I suppose it's more of a lair,' says Malcolm.

As my eyes adjust to the faint and flickering light, I look around the high wide space of the cave. My attention is drawn to three jars on a bench. I blink.

And I scream.

I scream long and loud and it takes me a good minute to . . . not calm down, exactly, but bring myself back from the brink of jabbering hysterics. I'm breathing hard, my heart is hammering against my ribs, and my eyes dance around the room from one ghastly object to the next. If they could, I think my eyes would simply pop themselves out of my head and roll away to whimper in the corner.

I glance again at the three glass jars.

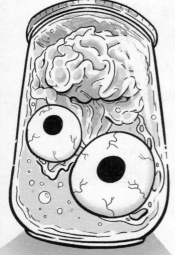

And I do the only thing that makes any sense.

I scream again.

'Bob,' says Lori's voice. 'Calm down. Everything is going to be OK.'

'OK? How is any of this OK? I feel like I'm losing my mind.'

'We know how you feel,' says Future Me, laughing.

Although how he says it, how he laughs, is something of a mystery. What with him having no mouth. What with him having no head. What with him being – basically – a brain and a pair of eyeballs floating in a jar of blue gloopy liquid.

Future Malcolm and my future girlfriend have also had their brains and eyes transferred from their heads into jars.

'You have no lips,' I say, somewhat obviously.

'We don't have much of anything,' says Future Me.

'How are you talking?'

'Blu-gloop,' says Future Me's voice. 'This liquid we're floating in is some kind of neuro-conductive matrix.'

'Translates our thoughts into a digital sequence,' says Malcolm's voice.

'Pipes them through that speaker,' says Lori, her eyes swivelling in the direction of a wooden box sitting on the bench.

There are no labels on the jars, but it's easy enough to guess which brain is which.

The bodies are standing behind the jars. They are all as still as statues, hollow eyed and brainless.

Zombies, you might say.

The lights in the cave gives the brainless bodies a cold, blue complexion, which only adds to the zombie effect. Whoever placed them here – Eno, I guess – has arranged the bodies in a series of ridiculous poses. Future Zombie Brainless Me has one hand on his hip and the other jutting out from his side, as if he had recently been singing that song about a little teapot, short and stout. Zombie Malcolm is sucking his thumb, and my future zombie girlfriend has her mouth open wide and her hands pressed to her cheeks as if she is screaming. Which, considering what's happened to them all, she probably was.

As if this wasn't weird enough, all three have had their heads shaved (to help get the brains out, I assume), and they are all wearing hospital gowns – the ones that fasten at the back leaving your bottom bare. I know this is probably the least of everybody's concerns, but I'm really hoping Eno left their underwear on.

A spider crawls up Malcolm's neck and settles in his beard. It looks kind of cosy there.

'What's that?' says Malcolm. 'On my face?'

'You can feel that?' I ask.

'Eno wired us up so we can't move but we can feel everything,' says Future Me.

As if it knows it's being talked about, the spider emerges from Malcolm's beard and walks slowly across his lips.

'It's a spider, isn't it?' says Malcolm.

I nod.

'Get it off!!!!' he shouts. 'Get. It. Off!!!!'

'What with?'

'I don't know. Your hand?'

'No way,' I say. 'It's massive.'

The spider extends a skinny leg towards one of Malcolm's nostrils.

Malcolm's brain shrieks, 'Do something!!! Won't you please do something!!'

I screw up my eyes and swipe in the general direction of Malcolm's face. The cave echoes with the sound of a loud slap.

'Ouch!' says Malcolm. 'Careful.'

I open one eye and see that Malcolm's face is spider free. Although it does have a red hand-shaped mark across the cheek.

'Has it gone?'

'It's gone,' I say. 'So, how about someone explains what the absolute heck is going on here?'

'Look behind you,' says the distorted voice of Future Me.

What I see when I turn around is an armchair, set in the centre of a gleaming metal cage. Attached to the bars of the cage are dozens of clocks, egg-timers, watches, hourglasses, sundials and other unusual devices with ticking bits and moving parts.

'What is it?'

'He's building a time machine,' says Future Me. 'And he's using my brain to power it.'

'Trying to,' says Future Malcolm. 'It hasn't worked so far.'

'Although last Thursday did seem to drag on for an awfully long time,' says my future girlfriend.

'Wait a moment,' I say. 'Why has he got you two pickled?' I glance at Malcolm and Lori. 'You're not time travellers.'

'Just for fun,' says Malcolm.

'Fun! That's . . . that's terrible. It's horrible. It's . . . evil.'

'That does tend to be an issue with evil geniuses,' says my future girlfriend.

'Some genius,' I say. 'He can't even make his time machine work.'

'He's close,' says Future Malcolm. 'Just needs to find one more . . . piece . . . to complete the circuit.'

'Piece? What piece?'

And three sets of eyes swivel sideways.

At the end of the bench is one more glass jar, full of fluid, but empty of brains or eyes.

'He needs one more brain,' says my future self.

And three sets of eyes swivel towards me.

'What? Wait! No! Me?'

'Yes,' says Future Me. 'You.'

'We need to stop him,' I say.

'Agreed,' says Future Me. 'Which means you need to get out of here. And pronto.'

'Get back to your own time and figure out another way to stop Eno,' says Lori.

'Ideally one that doesn't involve Lori telling him 'you're a time traveller,' says Future Malcolm.

'Sorry,' says Lori. 'It just slipped out.'

'And maybe steer clear of Mrs Gren's biology

classroom,' says Future Me. 'Don't want Eno getting any more ideas about things in jars.'

'I can't leave you all like this.'

'Very honourable,' says Future Me. 'But unless you've just taken a crash course in brain surgery, you don't have a choice.'

'Anyway,' says Lori. 'Once you go back and change the future, all this will no longer happen.'

'What if I make it worse?'

The three brains in jars laugh their spooky laughs. 'Hard to imagine what that would be,' says my future girlfriend.

Overhead a clock bongs. I turn in the direction of the sound just in time to see a wooden bird pop out of a little door set into the face of a cuckoo clock. The bird opens its beak and says:

'Intruder! Intruder! Intruder! Intruder! Intruder!'

THE PROBLEM WITH SMASHING YOUR OWN BRAINS IN. BISH BASH BOSH. SPIDERMAN UNDERPANTS. A REVOLTING HABIT.

The white overhead lights turn red now and start flashing in time with the cuckoo.

'Intruder! Intruder! Intruder! Intruder! Intruder!'

'Er, what's that all about?' I ask.

'It's an alarm clock,' says Future Malcolm. 'You've been detected.'

'Eno will be here any minute,' says Future Me. 'Time to go, Bob.'

'How? You know I can't control when I go. And there isn't a slide full of zombies for you to kick me down, so what do you suggest?'

'Intruder! Intruder! Intruder!'

'I want you to smash my brain jar,' says Future Me.

'Won't that . . . hurt?'

'It'll more than hurt,' chuckles Malcolm.

'You're asking me to drop my future brains on the floor?'

'Yes.'

'No. You'll . . . die.'

'It's the only way Bob. You – we – only ever travel to a place in time where some other version of ourselves exists. We're connected. That's how it works. That's why Eno needs you.'

'But –'

'With me . . . gone, the connection is broken and you should – fingers crossed – jolt back to the year 2023.'

'Fingers crossed? You don't even have fingers. I don't

like this plan. I don't like it one bit.'

'You'll like having your brains and eyes removed even less, trust me.'

'Intruder! Intruder! Intruder! Intruder! Intruder!'

'Bob!' says my future brain. 'Eno will be here any second. So pretty please, pick up the jar.'

'It's icky.'

'I know. I'm in it. Now get a grip and get on with it.'

The way my plaster cast is fitted, I can still use my fingers and thumb. It's not easy, but I manage to lift the jar from the table.

'Huh,' I say. 'It's lighter than I would have thought.'

'Well, maybe try harder at school when you get back,' says Future Me in a slightly wounded tone of voice. 'Now, if you would be so kind, please smash my brains out.'

I raise the jar above my head, feel its weight, ready myself to throw it on the ground and redecorate the cave floor in a lovely shade of my-brain pink . . .

. . . and then I put the jar back down on the bench.

'Bob,' says my future brain. 'What are you doing?'

'I can't do it. I can't just smash my own brains in.'

'This is bigger than us,' says my thirty-one-year-old brain. 'This is –'

'I know, I know. The future of all humanity et cetera. But there has to be another way!'

'Intruder! Intruder! Intruder! Intruder! Intruder!'

'If there was, don't you think we'd have thought of it?'

'I could hide,' I say. 'Then, you know, bash Eno over the head with a clock or something. I'll get the tingles, zip back to the past, change the future, bish bash bosh and happily ever after.'

'Bish bash bosh?' says Malcolm. 'That's your plan, is it? Bish bash bosh?'

'It's brilliant,' says Future Me.

'It is?' I say, slightly surprised.

'Yes,' says Future Me. 'It's simple and childlike and

perfect. Like hide and seek, but with the future of the world at stake.'

'And I like the bashing on the head part,' says Lori. 'That could work.'

'Intruder! Intruder!' says the cuckoo clock.

A clunk, a thunk, the sound of a lock turning.

All eyes – both in jars and in my head – turn towards the heavy wooden door at the far end of the cave.

'Well, if you're going to hide,' says Future Me, 'now would be a pretty good time to do it.'

I look around the huge and open space of the cave for a suitable hiding place – a wide pillar, a wardrobe, a pair of heavy curtains, a child-sized wicker basket. But – this being a cave – there are none of those things. Just lots and lots of wide-open space.

And three brainless bodies.

They're my best hope – my only hope – of somewhere to hide.

The sound of more locks turning. And say what you

will about Eno, he takes cave security very seriously.

I hurry over to the three bodies.

Teapot-styled Future Me stands with his legs wide apart, and it's clear I won't be able to hide behind him. Lori – forget about it. It wouldn't matter if she was ten feet tall and wearing a tent, there is no way I'm hiding behind a future girlfriend I have only just met. Especially one wearing a hospital gown.

Malcolm, on the other hand, is huge. Wide shouldered, broad chested, and with legs like small tree trunks.

The door at the far side of the cave creaks, and a man steps through the doorway and into the light.

Eno.

I dive behind Malcolm's body and crouch down behind his legs. It's a long way from perfect, but at least – thank the heavens – he is still wearing his underpants. A pair of Spiderman Y-fronts with a big Spiderman eye on each bum cheek.

'Careful there,' whispers Malcolm's brain. 'I'm ticklish.'

'Shh!' whispers Future Me.

Eno's footsteps echo across the floor. 'Little Robert Trebor,' he says. 'How nice of you to join us.'

Peeping between Malcolm's legs, I watch Eno approaching. He's older now and taller, but still with the same self-satisfied gloating expression on his face. The same smug tone in his voice.

'Come out and say hello, Bob. We have so much catching up to do.'

'What are you on about?' says Future Me's brain. 'He's not here.'

'Intruder! Intruder!' squawks the clock.

'My cuckoo begs to differ,' smarms Eno.

'Maybe your clock's faulty,' says Lori.

'Gone cuckoo,' laughs Malcolm.

'The only faulty thing around here,' says Eno, 'is your grasp on the seriousness of this situation.'

Eno has drawn level with the bench now, and squats down suddenly, peering underneath it, looking, presumably, for me. My heart is thumping and I should be feeling the tingles. But the only thing I feel is terrified.

'Don't forget,' says Eno, strolling around the table and approaching the zombified bodies, 'you may be reduced to three rather small brains in jars, but I can still make your lives very uncomfortable.'

Eno stands in front of Future Me. 'How long can you hold your breath, Trebor? Shall we find out?' And he places one hand over Future Me's mouth and uses the other to pinch his nostrils closed.

'Leave him!' shouts Lori's brain.

'It's fine,' replies my future brain, 'I can hold it for ages.'

'Where is he?' says Eno.

'Who?' says Future Me's brain. 'I don't know what you're talking about.'

From my position behind Malcolm's body, I see

the spider I swiped at earlier. It's sitting at the top of Future Me's back, and as I watch, it begins climbing up and over his left shoulder. Curious, perhaps, to see what all the fuss is about.

The spider crawls up onto Future Me's shoulder.

There is a pause.

And then Eno screams.

He screams like an opera singer who has just dropped a bowling ball on their foot.

Like a child who has seen a pair of eyes blinking at them from inside a wardrobe.

Like a man who is very very afraid of spiders.

Eno jumps back from my future body. My future body draws a breath.

Future Me laughs, Malcolm laughs, Lori laughs and it's all I can do not to laugh too.

Eno shakes himself. 'We'll see who has the last laugh,' he says. And he cracks the index finger of his left hand.

'Eeugh!' says Malcolm's brain. 'That really is a revolting habit.'

'Oh,' says Eno. ''Offends you, does it?'

He grips another finger. Pulls and twists. Kkrakkk!!!

'Urghh!' says Malcolm.

'Fine,' says Eno. 'I promise not to crack my knuckles.'

'Thank you,' says Malcolm.

'I'll crack yours instead,' and he grabs one of Malcolm's big fat fingers.

'Don't,' says Malcolm.

'Then tell me where the boy is.'

'Don't know what you're talking about.'

Eno yanks on Malcolm's finger.

Kreecccc!!!

'Fiend!' shouts Malcolm.

I can see Eno's feet through the gap in Malcolm's legs. It occurs to me that I could stamp on his toes, but I'm not sure that would be enough to stop him. Even if I stamped really hard. But . . .

I could tie his shoelaces together.

'Where – is – the boy?' demands Eno.

'What boy?' says Malcolm.

Kurrrick!!!

While Eno is busy pulling Malcolm's fingers, I begin the business of untying the right shoelace. He's tied it super tight, and – as my future self has already pointed out – I'm a fingernail biter. I can't get the knot loose.

Nothing else for it, I poke my head between Malcolm's legs and use my teeth to loosen his shoelace. It tastes revolting, but it's working – the damp, mouldy-smelling lace begins to untangle.

'Eight more fingers to go,' says Eno. 'Now – where – is – the boy?'

'Boy? What boy?'

Crrukkk! goes Malcolm's finger.

'Noooo!' goes Malcolm's brain.

Eno's first lace is undone now and I quickly turn my attention, and my mouth, to the next.

With both laces untied, I start fastening them together into a tangled knot that – come to think of it – looks rather like a tiny black brain.

'Seven,' says Eno, gripping Malcolm's middle finger.

'I wouldn't do that if I were you,' says Malcolm.

'Really?' says Eno, amused. 'Well, you're not me, are you?'

And he pulls the finger.

If it cracks or not, I can't say.

Because any sound is drowned out by an enormous rippling fart.

20

NOWHERE TO HIDE.
BI-DODAH-WHATNOTS.
NOT SMILING NOW.
BRAIN SKIDS.

It's a huge, echoing foghorn of a fart. A tremendous trumpet of a trouser toot. A booming bass drum of a bottom blast. I feel the hot wind of it ruffling my hair and billowing down the back of my shirt.

'Malcolm!' I shriek. 'That is disgusting!!'

'He pulled my finger,' Malcolm says. 'I c ouldn't resist!'

Cabbages, parsnips, old bacon, mouldy cheese and farmer's feet – the smell hits me like a punch on the nose and a knee in the guts. I jump to my feet so quickly

I accidentally head-butt the Schnitz between the legs.

'Yeeeeowwwwch!' his brain screams. 'Right in the futures.'

Future Eno, it seems, still likes to smirk. He does it now. 'Welcome to the party, Bob. Any last requests before I remove your brain?'

'I don't suppose you'd mind putting everybody back together, then throwing yourself off the nearest cliff?'

'You suppose correctly, Trebor.' Eno flexes his fingers and cracks his knuckles.

I back away from the evil maniac, coming to a sudden stop when my hip bumps against the bench, making the brain jars rattle.

Eno regards me with an amused and thoroughly evil smile.

'There's nowhere to hide, little boy.'

I really should be feeling the tingles by now, but while my pulse is racing, my body is worryingly tingle-free.

'Don't take one step towards me,' I say. 'Or you'll be sorry.'

Eno sniggers. 'Really?'

'Really.'

He's about to take a step, then he stops, he hesitates. And I realise my mistake.

I was so pleased with myself for tying his laces together, that I couldn't resist a sneaky glance at my handiwork. But apparently my sneaky glance wasn't sneaky enough. Eno noticed, and now he looks down too. He sees the balled-up knot of his laces. And he smiles.

'Honestly,' he says. 'The old "tie their shoelaces together" routine. You seem to have forgotten you're dealing with a genius.'

Then he smiles and clicks the heels of his shoes together.

The tips of his shoelaces glow red, the knot quivers and comes undone. Then the ends of his unknotted laces rise like charmed snakes, they sway around each other and tie themselves into two nice neat bows. The tips of the laces flash green then blink out.

'What just happened?'

Eno grins. 'My self-securing footwear-closure system just happened, that's what.'

'Sorry, what?'

Eno sighs. 'Self-tying laces, you ignoramus.'

'Told you it was a good idea,' says Malcolm.

'Bob!' shouts my future brain. 'Plan A! Back to Plan A!'

'Plan A?' Eno and I say at the same time.

'Smash me,' says my brain. 'Smash me right now!'

'I would not advise you do that,' says Eno, moving towards me.

I snatch up the jar and hold it above my head. 'Stay away from me, you villain.'

'You wouldn't dare,' says Eno, advancing. 'Drop that brain and you both die.'

'He's lying,' says Future Me.

'And what would you know?' says Eno. 'I paid attention in biology lessons. All you did was make rude noises and draw pretend tattoos on your hands.'

'Don't listen to him,' says Future Me.

'But it's true,' I say. 'I'm rubbish at biology. I don't even know which side my lung is on.'

Eno takes another step towards me, and I take another step back.

'Drop it,' says my future brain.

'Don't,' says Eno.

I continue walking backwards, passing beneath the telltale cuckoo clock, which ticks, clicks and activates above my head.

'Intruder!' squawks the bird, springing from its hatch. 'Intruder!'

I back up one more step and my shoulders bump up against the cold cave wall. I'm trapped.

'I expect you're waiting for the tingles?' says Eno,

wiggling his fingers in the air.

I try to shrug, but that's not an easy thing to do with a jar full of brain above your head.

'You'll be waiting a long time,' says Eno. 'The "tingles"', as you call them, are bi-directional temporal oscillations.'

'Bi-dodah-whatnots?'

'Time-ripples,' says Eno. 'And that' – he points to the cuckoo clock above our heads – 'in addition to being an intruder alarm, is a time-ripple dampener. No ripples. No travel. And you triggered it five minutes ago when you materialised in my cave.'

'Actually,' says Future Me, 'he arrived fifteen minutes ago.'

Eno frowns, checks his watch then checks the time on the cuckoo clock. 'Blasted thing is running slow,' he says. 'Must need winding.'

'Ha! Not as smart as you think you are,' I say, smirking.

'Smart enough to remove your brain,' says Eno, and the smirk melts from my face.

'Not smiling now, are you?' says Eno, stepping closer.

I try to think of a clever comeback, but it seems I'm all out of clever. So I do the only thing left to me. I stick out my tongue and blow a big fat raspberry.

Eno grimaces. 'How utterly childish.'

'No,' I say. 'Not childish. Childlike. There's a big difference.'

'Yes, Bob!' shouts my future brain. 'Yes!'

'Enough,' says Eno. 'Let's get this over with.'

'Yes,' I say. 'Let's.'

I grip the brain jar, take careful aim at the cuckoo clock, and throw.

'Nooooooo!' says Eno.

'Intruder!' says the cuckoo clock.

'Sorry,' I say, as the jar containing my future brain smashes into Eno's time-ripple dampener.

'Shot!' shouts Malcolm's brain.

Cuckoo clock and jar crash to the floor in a mess of broken glass, clock springs, gloopy gel, brain and eyes. Eno whirls around, steps directly on my future brain, skids, falls and says a very rude word.

The clock is destroyed.

My brain is mush.

The tingles.

The drags.

Everything begins to fade away.

'I believe in you, Bob,' shouts Lori's brain. 'I believe in you.'

But her voice is fading to nothing.

And I am out of here.

THOSE FINGERS HAVE TOUCHED MY BRAIN. ENO LOSES HIS SMILE. DANCING QUEEN. SOMETHING THAT RHYMES WITH TAMBOURINE.

Eno is strutting about the room in his selfie hat – confident, smug, irritating.

He pushes his glasses up onto his nose, and while his fingers are in the area he picks a bogey from one nostril and wipes it on his trousers. It's not a pleasant sight. But the thing that's really grossing me out is this:

Those hands – those nose-picking, knuckle-cracking fingers – have held my brain!

'You should all go home now,' he says. 'It's a foregone conclusion that I'm going to win. You know, I wouldn't be surprised if the judges award me second and third places as well.'

He cracks his knuckles.

He poses for a selfie in front of his dangling phone.

At my side, Malcolm clenches his fists. 'I can't wait to smash that thing.'

'We can't,' I say. 'It's only going to make things worse.'

'Thought so,' says Dismal.

'Then why didn't you say so?'

Gloria shrugs. 'You seemed so determined.'

My tummy gurgles. 'Don't suppose you have any more of those pastries, do you?'

Gloria reaches into her bag. 'All gone,' she says. 'I've got a slice of banana bread.'

'Wait? What did you – did you just say . . . banana bread?'

Gloria gives me a strange look. 'Yes. Why? What's wrong with banana bread?'

This is all getting a bit loopy. 'Nothing, I suppose. I just . . . it's complicated,' I say. 'Really complicated.'

'It's really not,' says Gloria. 'Butter, sugar, eggs, flour, bananas. Simple. Do you want some or not?'

My tummy rumbles.

'I'll take that as a yes,' says Gloria, handing me a slice. I thank her with my eyes and take a big bite. The banana bread is moist, sweet and melt-in-the-mouth. It is, in a word, delicious. I finish it in one more bite.

'Blimey,' says Gloria. 'I've seen monkeys with better table manners.'

'Presumably they haven't just travelled twenty years into the future and twenty back without anything to eat,' I say.

'Ah,' says Malcolm. 'I thought you looked a bit pale.'

You would too if you'd just seen your brain in a jar, I think, but don't say.

'What happened?' says Gloria.

'Nothing good,' I tell her.

'Zombies?' asks Malcolm.

My mind flashes onto the image of Future Me, Future Malcolm and Lori – empty eyed and brainless. 'A few,' I say. 'Yes.'

'Anyone care for a photograph with this year's winner?' Eno says to the room.

I'd give just about anything to wipe that smug smile off his face. And as I think the thought, I remember the last thing Future Eno said before he stepped in my brains.

Well, the fourth-to-last thing, to be accurate. After calling me 'childish', insisting we 'get on with it', and yelling, 'Noooooo!'

The fourth-to-last thing Eno said before stepping on my brain was:

Not smiling now, are you?

And his words give me an idea. It's not going to save the world, but it might stop Eno swaggering around the place for ten minutes. And for now, that will have to do.

'I'll have a selfie,' I say.

Eno looks at me like I've just said I'd like to give him a massive hug. Which is to say, with a mixture of mistrust and disbelief.

'What are you playing at, Trebor?'

'Nothing,' I say, standing. 'Just want to see if your ridiculous invention works.'

'Of course it works, I'm a –'

'Yeah, yeah. A genius, Eno. So you keep saying.'

It's not every day you get to stand next to someone who's removed, handled and stepped in your brain, and standing next to Eno now, my scalp prickles. It's quite unpleasant.

'Right,' I say, 'how does this thing work?'

'You smile,' says Eno, not smiling. 'That's why it's called a smile-activated selfie hat.'

'But what if I don't want to smile? What if I just want to stand here and look . . . moody.'

'Moody? What do you mean moody?'

'Anything other than smiling. What if I want to look cool, sad, awkward, disgusted, bored, silly, funny. What if I want to look like a cross-eyed monkey?'

'Why would anyone want to look like that?' says Eno.

'For fun,' I shoot back. 'You know what fun is, don't you?'

'Of course I know what fun is, I'm a –'

'Yeah yeah, a genius. Well, hate to break it to you, Eno, but that silly thing stuck to your head is about as clever as a brick and as useful as a light-activated torch. And it is, trust me on this, no one's idea of fun.'

'But it's, you know, smile activated,' he says, a nd all the smug, all the self-satisfied smarm has left his voice. His head droops slightly, his phone bobbing pathetically on its bendy rod.

'Not smiling now, are you?' I say.

I go back to my friends.

And Eno slouches off to sit by himself in the corner.

'Ouch,' says Malcolm. 'That was brutal!'

'I know,' I say. 'I feel kind of bad for him.'

Maria Mamooli goes over to Eno, asking if he'd like to stroke one of her hamsters, and this small act of kindness makes me feel even worse about my own act of meanness.

Even if he did scoop my brain out.

'So,' says Malcolm. 'Now what?'

'We do the only thing we can,' says Gloria. 'We play.'

'In case you hadn't noticed,' I say, holding up my plaster cast, 'I have a broken arm. No arm, no drums. No drums, no Tentacles of Time.'

'One word,' says Gloria, reaching into her bag. 'Tambourine!'

And she rattles the silly thing right in my face.

'For the last time, Dismal, serious rock bands – hard rock bands – do not go about rattling tambourines!'

'Fine,' says Gloria. 'Then we'll be something else.'

'I don't want to be something else.'

Gloria gives me the kind of look parents give to sulky children who don't want to eat their vegetables.

'Do you want civilisation to be overrun with zombies?' she says, and her tone matches her look.

'No.'

'Right,' says Gloria, 'that's settled. Malcolm will play guitar, and I' – she gives her tambourine a shake – 'will play this.'

'What about me?'

'You,' says Gloria Dismal, 'will sing.'

'I abso-flipping-lutely won't!'

Gloria gives me the look again. The one that says, You will eat your vegetables, Robert. Every last mouthful. Otherwise, it's straight to bed with no pudding.

'I can't,' I say. 'I can't sing.'

'Yes, you can. I've heard you in the shower. And the way you sing "Dancing Queen" is really quite lovely.'

'Dancing Queen' was Mum's favourite song. She used to sing it in the car, in the kitchen, in the garden, and in the shower. And singing my mum's favourite song helps me remember her and feel close to her. Although I hadn't realised I had an audience.

The thought of Gloria listening to me sing ABBA songs is embarrassing enough. But the fact that she has been listening to me singing ABBA songs while I'm completely naked in the shower is enough to make me want to hide under the desk and wait for the zombie apocalypse to happen. I'm considering doing just that when Mr Huffman steps into the room to collect Jamal Smith – the first act in this year's Griffin's Got Talent.

And this is it – the show is about to start and the future of humanity hangs in the balance. It's time to get serious.

Jamal leaves with Mr Huffman, and a nervous hush falls about the room.

Malcolm is deep in thought. I don't say anything because it doesn't happen often and I don't want to break his concentration. Perhaps he's on the brink of coming up with a plan. Gloria senses this too, and the pair of us wait while Malcolm's mind does its thing.

He blinks. He turns to me, and he says:

'"Dancing Queen"? You were singing "Dancing Queen"?'

I laugh. 'What can I say? It's a great song. But I'm not singing it in front of that lot.'

'Good,' says Malcolm. 'Because I only know how to play three chords and I think two of them might be the same.'

'More than enough,' says Gloria, reaching into her bag. She produces a notebook with a sparkly cover and flicks through several pages before finding the one she wants. 'I've been working on a song I think you'll like.'

Malcolm and I exchange a quick glance. But that quick glance says a great deal. It says: I find it highly unlikely we will like your song, Gloria Dismal, but we're in a pinch, here, so let's just cross our fingers and hope for the best.

Gloria is staring intently at her notebook. Her lips are moving, but they make no sound.

'So,' I say. 'Are you going to share this song?'

'I would,' says Gloria, 'but it's not finished.'

She says this with no sense of panic. As if we had weeks instead of minutes to prepare. As if the only thing at stake was a few pounds' worth of shopping vouchers, not the fate of the entire world.

'Jamal Smith is on stage right now!' I say. 'In a few minutes, it'll be Jeremy Dither. And after that it's save-the-world-from-zombies time. It's kind of a big deal.'

'I am aware of this,' says Gloria, pulling a biro from somewhere in the depths of her hair. 'And I'm working on it. I just need a word that rhymes with tambourine.'

'Of course you do,' I say. 'I mean, what else would it possibly be?'

'Don't try and be sarcastic,' says Gloria, 'you're rubbish at it. Now' – she taps her watch with the tip of her pen – 'something that rhymes with tambourine.'

'Tangerine,' says Malcolm.

'No,' says Gloria.

'Aubergine?'

'No food,' says the Dismal.

'Why not?'

'Because.'

'Jelly bean,' tries Malcolm.

'Still food,' says Dismal.

'Sunscreen?'

'Nope.'

'Guillotine?'

'Absolutely not.'

'Time machine,' I say.

Gloria's eyes light up. 'Yes! Bob Trebor, I could kiss you.'

'No, you could not,' I say.

But Gloria isn't listening, she's writing in her notebook. She chews the top of her pen. Crosses something out. Writes something in its place. And then she smiles and pushes the biro back into the tangle of her hair.

'Finished,' she says, passing the piece of paper to me. 'I'd say you've got about eight minutes to learn it before we have to go on stage and save the world.'

'A whole eight?' I say.

Gloria smiles. 'Loads of time.'

Einstein And The Rolling Stones

My favourite album is Forty Licks, which is all the greatest hits by the Rolling Stones. It lasts for two hours, thirty-five minutes and fifty-two seconds.

My least favourite subject in the whole world is physics. A lesson lasts for fifty minutes exactly.

When I listen to Forty Licks, time flies.

When I sit at the back of Mr Huffman's windowless classroom, time drags like a bag of bricks.

The Rolling Stones album is one hour, forty-five minutes and fifty-two seconds longer than the physics lesson. But the physics lesson feels about ten thousand years longer.

Time, you see, is not fixed. Time is tricky.

I think this is what Albert Einstein was going on about in his famous theory of relativity. But I can't be sure because I wasn't paying attention when old Huffy tried to explain it to us.

Why do I mention this?

Because no sooner had Gloria Dismal passed me the lyrics to her song, than old Huffy was walking into the room to call the Tentacles of Time (plus tambourine) onto the stage.

It was the fastest eight minutes I've ever known.

NAKED BENEATH THE LIGHTS.
A TAMBOURINE AFTER ALL.
ONE TWO,
A ONE TWO THREE FOUR.

It's brighter than I'd imagined up here. The lights above the stage are shining directly into our eyes and it's almost impossible to make out the faces of the audience. And that's a good thing. This way I can pretend there's no one there. I can pretend I'm at home, singing in the shower.

Well, almost.

The sound of Gloria's tinkling tambourine is a clear reminder that I am not standing beneath a stream of hot water, but on a stage in front of several hundred people. And while I may not be naked beneath these lights, I certainly feel as though I am.

Gloria counts us in.

'One two, a one two three four.'

I open my mouth and sing.

SHAKE IT LIKE A TAMBOURINE

Lyrics: Dizamale and Trebor

They said you can't rock with a tambourine
But I have seen the future
And we can do whatever we please
Even if it's not what you're used ta.

So don't be a zombie and follow the crowd
That would be a bad scene
Instead you gotta write your own history
And shake it up like a tambourine.

Shake it up, shake it up, shake it one more time
Now tell me, do you know what I mean?
Shake it up, shake it up, shake it two more times
And shake it like a tambourine.

Don't bob alone like a brain in a jar
That would be a disaster
Like jumping up and down on a trampoline
With a belly full of cheesy pasta.

If you make a big mess, don't forget
Life is like a time machine
Every day begins a bright new future
So shake it up like a tambourine.

Shake it up, shake it up, shake it one more time
Now tell me, do you know what I mean?
Shake it up, shake it up, shake it two more times
And shake it like a tambourine.

[CONTINUED]

A FINAL TINKLE.
APPLAUSE.
A TEAM.
A HUG.

The final note from Malcolm's guitar echoes above the audience.

Gloria lowers her tambourine in a final tinkle.

I swallow, and the sound is loud inside my ringing ears.

The hall is otherwise silent.

And I am so – so – thankful for these blinding lights.

Then the clapping starts. Hundreds of hands coming together in wild applause. Feet stamping. Cheering. Whistling. And more clapping.

'I think they liked it,' says Malcolm.

I turn to Gloria. 'You're a genius,' I tell her.

'No,' she says. 'We're a team.'

'A gang,' I say. 'A squad, a crew, tribe, troop, posse.'

What Gloria does next is something I have never seen her do before – she looks embarrassed. And then she hugs me. She pushes her cheek close to mine, and whispers, 'Thank you.'

In front of the whole blinking school.

I get the tingles.

I get the drags.

I travel twenty years forward in time.

THE LAST BOUNCE.
A NOT-EXACTLY-KIND-OF
TIME MACHINE.
BOB MEETS HIS FUTURE GIRLFRIEND.
DID I JUST SEE A GIANT HAMSTER?

Malcolm screams.

But it's just a little one. It's really more of a squeak than a scream.

And it's such a huge relief to see them both – Malcolm and Future Me – with their brains and eyeballs restored to their proper places, that I laugh out loud.

'So it's . . . it's true?' says Malcolm.

Future Me nods. 'Every word.'

'You warned him I'd be coming?' I say.

'The best I could,' says Future Me.

'Time travel,' says Malcolm. 'It's . . . impossible. Isn't it?'

'We talked about this earlier,' says Future Me.

'So did we,' I add.

Malcolm looks from one of us to the other. Like he always does.

'It's one thing talking about it,' he says. 'It's something else watching it actually happen at the kitchen table.'

As Malcolm says, I have landed back in the kitchen, squarely in a seat in front of the table. A freshly baked and perfectly formed banana bread sits between us. Steam rises from the loaf, bringing with it the cosy aroma of real bananas, sugar, butter, and . . . something I can't quite identify.

'Pecans?' says Future Me. 'Thought I'd change it up a bit this time.'

'This time,' says Malcolm, shaking his head. 'How? How does it work?'

I shake my head. 'No idea. You?' I ask, turning to my future self.

'Nothing solid,' he says. 'But I think this' – he pulls back his sleeve to show his Mickey Mouse watch – 'might have something to do with it.'

'Your watch is a time machine?' says Malcolm.

Future Me laughs. 'No. Well, not exactly. Kind of, maybe.'

'You're losing me,' I say.

'Not the watch exactly,' says Future Me. 'But what it stands for. It keeps me connected to my younger self.'

'To me?' I say, glancing at my own version of the same watch.

'I carry you inside me,' says Future Me. 'You're a part of me. But as I get older, that eleven-year-old boy gets buried under all the layers of growing up. So I do my best to stay young. To remember the boy I was. To keep him . . . present, I suppose. I think that connection is part of what pulls us through the years to some older version of ourselves. And I think that's why the travel only works in one direction.'

'I don't understand,' I say.

'You travel forward, because I've carried you with me into the future. A part of you is already here.' He taps his chest and winks. 'But in your time – in 2023 – the older me hasn't formed, hasn't happened, and that, I think, is why I can't travel to you.'

'That's why you keep the toys,' I say. 'And wear the silly clothes.'

'I'll ignore that last comment, Bob. But yes. I told you – it's important to remain childlike.'

I put my hands to the sides of my head and mime my brain exploding. I even do the sound effects: 'Kkpppwwwffffffff! Mind. Blown. And you figured this out yourself?'

Future Me shakes his head. 'I'm not that smart.'

'So how? Who?'

'I heard it from fifty-year-old me. You'd like him. Bit strange. But nice.'

'And who told him?'

'Ah, well, he got it from sixty-two-year-old him. Sixty-two-year-old us.'

'And I suppose he got it from seventy-something-year-old us?'

'Exactly,' says Future Me. 'And so on.'

'Surely there's more to it than acting like a child,' says Malcolm. 'Otherwise the world would be full of time travellers.'

'Very true,' says Future Me. 'It's only a very small part of a bigger picture. Like the electricity in a flying car.'

'Or the banana in a loaf?' I say, and my stomach gurgles.

Future Me laughs. 'Well said, young me.'

'I don't suppose I could have a slice?'

'Patience,' he says. 'Lori will be here in' – he checks

in with Mickey Mouse – 'less than five minutes.'

'So,' I say, trying not to think about the delicious, warm, sweet-smelling cake. 'What's the zombie situation?'

Future Me smiles. 'No zombies.'

'Honestly? We won Griffin's Got Talent?'

Malcolm shakes his head. 'Jamal won.'

I nod thoughtfully. 'He was good.'

'Exactly,' says Malcolm. 'We came a close second. No shame coming second to an expert spoon player like Jamal.'

'And Eno?'

'Came last,' says Future Me. 'He lost all his confidence after that talking-to you gave him in Mr Huffman's room. He could hardly raise a smile by the time he walked on stage, and when he did manage one it was so forced his selfie hat wouldn't work. It was painful to watch.'

I know it was done for the good of civilisation as

we know it, but I feel kind of rotten.

Future Me punches me lightly on the shoulder. 'You did what needed to be done,' he says. 'Plus, things worked out pretty well for Eno.'

'Fell in love with Maria Mamooli,' says Malcolm. 'They breed hamsters now.'

'Hamsters?! Is this some kind of joke?'

'Not at all,' says Malcolm. 'Hamsters are . . .'

'Big,' says Future Me, laughing. 'Really big.'

And Malcolm laughs too, even though the 'joke' isn't remotely funny.

'And the band?' I say. 'Are we – are you – still together?'

'Still rockin',' says Future Me.

'Still not famous,' says Malcolm.

'Don't look so disappointed,' says Future Me. 'You saved the world, remember. We all did.'

'You'd think something like that might deserve a slice of cake,' I say. And my tummy rumbles in agreement.

The doorbell rings.

Future Me smiles, 'She's here.'

Sitting next to the banana bread is a small black box, which Future Me now opens. From the box he removes an impressive diamond ring, which he then pushes through the surface of the cake, burying it finger deep somewhere in the middle.

'I hope you washed your hands,' I say.

Future Me licks the cake off his finger and goes to answer the door.

I can't see the door from where we're sitting, but I can hear Bob and Lori talking in hushed voices.

I glance at Malcolm, and he offers me a reassuring smile. 'Don't worry,' he says. 'You'll like her.'

'I'll be the judge of that,' I tell him.

'Just . . . be nice,' says Malcolm. 'And . . . try not to freak out.'

In the hallway I hear a long wet sucky kind of sound. I can think of three possibilities. Either:

My future self has fallen into a badly planned indoor swamp.

He has been attacked by a pet octopus.

He is kissing Lori.

Lori . . .

There's something about the name nagging at a far corner of my brain. Presumably it's short for something, but what?

Loris, Floris, Dolores . . . ?

Another wet squelchy sound suggests that either the octopus has followed Bob into the swamp, or my future self has finally removed his lips from those of my future fiancée. I hear footsteps, which kind of rules out the octopus-swamp thing.

And here it comes, I'm about to meet my future girlfriend, and my future self is about to ask her to marry him. I feel stressed for both of us. For all three of us, actually.

Future Me walks into the kitchen, the lady he is

about to propose to close behind and holding his hand.

'Bob,' says Future Me. 'Meet Lori.'

Lori is tall, with long legs that make up around three quarters of her body. She has curly hair and an amused smile.

'Hey, Bob,' she says. 'I believe we've met before.'

And she does look familiar. Awfully familiar.

'Lori?' I say. 'Is that . . . short for something?'

Lori smiles. 'That's right,' says my future fiancée. 'It's short for –'

'Gloria,' I say. 'Gloria Dismal.'

And Gloria laughs. 'Surprise!'

'Wait a minute,' I say. 'When we met in Eno's cave, you said I didn't know you.'

'I remember,' says Gloria with a gentle laugh.

'But I live next door to you. You vomited on my trampoline. You helped me save the world.'

'All true, but there's more to me than that, Bob. What's my favourite song? My biggest fear, my wildest dream, my favourite thing to eat?'

I shrug, mildly embarrassed about how little I really know about Gloria.

'Getting to know someone,' she says, 'to really know them – takes time.'

'Luckily,' says Future Me, 'that's something you've got plenty of.'

And then Gloria goes and kisses me on the cheek.

My skin prickles with goosebumps, the hairs stand up on the back of my neck, and it looks like I won't be getting a slice of banana bread after all.

'Tingles?' says Future Me, and all I can do is nod.

'Oh no,' says Gloria. 'So soon?'

And here come the drags – heavy and warm and unstoppable.

'Take care of yourself,' says Future Me. 'Eat some vegetables, brush your teeth and . . . don't be in a hurry to grow up.'

'I'll do my best,' I say with a smile.

And I think we both know – both feel – that this is the final bounce of this particular trip.

My vision starts to blur, but not before something truly bizarre catches my eye. Outside the kitchen window, a woman passes by, walking what appears to be a huge fluffy dog. But this is bigger than any dog I've seen before – this is the size of a donkey. And it's not exactly dog-shaped. It's rounder. Like an enormous pom-pom. Like – in fact – an enormous hamster. But surely it can't be.

Can it?

And then I'm gone.

24

STILL HUNGRY.
AS IF, ROBERT TREBOR.
AND THE WINNER IS . . .
FINALLY, SOME CAKE.

Hundreds of hands clapping, feet stamping, voices cheering. All for me, Malcolm and Gloria Dismal, who, I will one day – apparently, impossibly, unbelievably – ask to marry me. It's a lot to wrap an eleven-year-old head around.

And I'm still hungry.

'I think they liked it,' says Malcolm.

The last time I was here, I told Gloria she was a genius, and for all I know that might have been the first step towards us becoming – I can barely form the words inside my head – boyfriend and girlfriend. The thought crosses my mind that if I don't compliment her now, I could change the future, I could stop all that horrible romantic nonsense. But . . . Future Me seemed so happy. And who am I to interfere in his life, in his future?

'What?' says Gloria, and I realise I am staring at her.

What the heck.

'You're a genius,' I tell her.

Gloria's eyes sparkle. 'No,' she says. 'We're a team.'

'A gang,' I say. 'A squad, a crew, tribe, troop, posse.'

Gloria beams.

'Just don't try and hug me,' I say.

Gloria pulls a face. 'As if, Robert Trebor.'

But she looks a little embarrassed when she says it.

The crowd are still clapping, but the energy is fading, and our time in the spotlight is coming to an end.

As predicted by Future Me and Future Malcolm, the Tentacles of Time came second in Griffin's Got Talent.

'Jamal really was excellent,' says Gloria. And none of us disagree.

'Maybe we should ask him to join the band?' says Malcolm.

'I'm still getting used to the tambourine,' I tell him. 'I don't think I'm ready for cutlery.'

'Right,' says Malcolm. 'Probably best.'

And for a quiet moment, the three of us sit on the front steps of the school, watching people come and go, completely unaware of the fate they have so narrowly escaped.

'Still,' says Schnitzel, 'second place and fifteen pounds' worth of vouchers ain't bad.'

'And we saved the world,' says Gloria. 'Didn't we?'

'We did,' I say.

But I say no more, because the future is a delicate thing, and the less anyone else knows about it the better. Particularly as it might involve a wedding. And some giant hamsters.

'So,' says Schnitzel, 'what will we spend the vouchers on?'

'What's your favourite thing to eat?' I ask Gloria.

'Oh, that's easy. Iced cinnamon buns with cherries on top.'

'In that case,' I say, 'how about we go to the bakery and blow our vouchers on cake?'

'That,' says Gloria, 'is the best idea you've had all day.'

AFTER

A GRAVEYARD.
A PREGNANT GHOST.
THE BABY I WAS.
TINGLE-WINGLES.

Some days after school, when the weather is nice, or at least not too horrible, I go to the graveyard, sit on the short wooden bench near Mum's grave and say hello. Sometimes, I bring Zem. He likes to chase the squirrels that live in the trees here.

The bench has a little brass plaque screwed onto the back that says:

in memory of anna trebor – loving wife and mother.

It's set close to a wall, under the shade of a very old sycamore tree, which drops propeller-shaped seeds in the autumn. As well as Mum's grave, you can see all of the graveyard from this bench. The rows of old stones and plots, some fresh and marked with flowers, others long overgrown with the carved names on the headstones smoothed away with time.

Why I mention this – the position of Mum's bench, the wall at its back, the view over the cemetery – is that there's no way anyone could creep up on me here. I'd see them coming. Unless, I suppose, they slowly lowered themselves out of the sycamore branches above my head.

I mention this because five minutes ago, there wasn't a lady sitting on the bench beside me.

And now there is.

Plus, she is heavily pregnant, which pretty much rules out the idea of her dropping silently out of the sycamore tree.

I should probably be terrified, what with this being a graveyard and everything. But I'm not. Something about this lady is familiar. If anything, I feel more at ease with her beside me.

'Hello,' she says.

'Hello,' I say, pointing my chin towards Mum's grave. 'Did you know her?'

The lady nods. 'You've got your father's eyes,' she says. And I notice her own eyes are wet with tears. 'How is he?'

'He's OK,' I say. 'He misses Mum.'

The lady wipes her eyes with a handkerchief. 'I miss him too,' she says. 'I miss you both.'

To say I realise only now that this lady is my mother wouldn't be entirely right. I think I knew from the moment I first noticed her. She's younger than the Mum I remember – about ten years younger at a guess – but her eyes, her smile, her voice and her smell are all familiar. But it's more than this; it's . . . it's a feeling. A connection, maybe.

'Mum?'

The lady nods. She pats her pregnant tummy and says, 'You've grown.'

As with all of these situations, it's a lot to take in.

'Are you . . . do you travel?'

'Yes. I'm like you. And before me, your grandfather travelled too.'

'Does Dad know?'

'He knows.'

'But you never told me. Neither of you ever told me.'

'We were going to,' she says. 'We were waiting for the right time, and then . . .' Mum's eyes flick towards her grave.

'I'm sorry,' I say, and now my eyes are all teary too.

'Oh sweetheart,' Mum says, and she holds out a hand to me. 'Don't be sorry.'

But she doesn't know what I'm apologising for. She's too young to know what a brat I was on my eleventh birthday when she gave me a present I didn't care for. She doesn't know that after that, she walked into the village. And she doesn't know about the freak accident that took her from me and Dad and brought her here, to this plot in the cemetery.

'I know,' Mum says, as if reading my thoughts. 'And it wasn't your fault.'

'What do you mean? It hasn't happened to you yet.'

'I remember my entire life,' Mum says. 'Including the bits that haven't happened yet. I remember you being born, your first Christmas, first tooth, first word. I remember watching you sleep at night in your daddy's arms. I remember everything.'

'I don't understand.'

Mum laughs, 'I'm not sure I do, either. 'But I think it has something to do with me being, you know, sort of dead.'

'Sort of?' I say.

'Well, I'm sitting here talking to you, aren't I?'

'Did you travel here?'

Mum squints up at the sycamore tree, as if looking

for the answer to my question in the tangle of branches. 'Not exactly,' she says. 'You travel now?'

I nod. 'Yesterday actually.'

'Was it fun?'

'It was . . . weird,' I say. 'It was very weird.'

'Yeah,' she says with a knowing smile. 'It tends to be.'

'So how are you here?'

'You know when you go,' Mum says, 'how one minute you're somewhere – then, with me, anyway, my skin gets ticklish –'

'The tingles,' I say.

'That's right. But I always called them the shudders. And then I get the squashers.'

'The drags,' I say. 'I call them the drags.'

Mum chuckles at this. 'Well, before I came here today, I wasn't . . . anywhere. No tingles, no drags. I don't think I came from the past, exactly. I think I came from . . . somewhere else, if you know what I mean.'

'But how?'

'My guess is, you brought me. Or, to be more precise, him.'

'The baby?'

Mum nods as she rubs her hand in a slow circle over her tummy. And then she winces like she's in pain. 'You're kicking,' she says. 'Do you want to feel?'

I'm not sure that I do. It's weird. But at the same time, I am curious.

Mum takes my hand and places it on her round belly. For a moment, nothing happens, and then I feel a tiny prod – a kick – against the palm of my hand.

'I don't think we have long left,' Mum says. 'I think this little chap has the tingles.'

And then she says it again to her belly, in that high-pitched voice people use when they're talking to babies.

'Does somebody have the tingle-wingles? Yes you do. Yes you do.'

'But I don't travel till I'm eleven,' I say to Mum. 'Till the day after . . . after you . . .'

'I was twelve when I first travelled,' Mum says. 'It's hard work; you need to be strong enough for it to happen. But I think, maybe because he's in my tummy, maybe I can give him the strength he needs.'

'But why here? Why now?'

'We travel to our future selves,' Mum says. 'You're his future self. And my future self is . . .' she looks across to her grave, 'over there.'

'So you're not going back? To whenever it was you were like this?'

Mum shakes her head. 'I don't think it works like that. Not for me. Not now.'

'Are you . . .' the word I want to say seems silly.

'A ghost?' says Mum.

I nod.

'Honest answer, sweetheart – I don't know. I don't feel like a ghost. And this little chap certainly isn't – ghosts don't kick like he does. I think I'm more like a ripple in a pond. I don't know, Bob – maybe that's exactly what a ghost is.'

Mum winces again, both hands going to her tummy this time.

'Goodness,' she says. 'I always hated drags.'

'You're going?'

'But I'll be back.'

'I'll come again tomorrow,' I say. 'I'll come every day.'

'No,' says Mum, shaking her head. 'Promise me you won't do that.'

I say nothing.

'Bob, who knows when I'll be back again? It might be years, and I don't want you wasting your time waiting around in a graveyard. Life is for living, Bob. Also, people will think you're weird.'

'I am weird.'

Mum laughs. 'Let's call it special, shall we? Now promise – no hanging around in the graveyard.'

'OK,' I say. 'I promise.'

'Just come when the mood takes you,' Mum says. 'Give it . . . you know, time.'

My eyes are blurring now, but this isn't the tingles. Tears are falling down my cheeks and there's nothing I can do to stop them.

'Talk to Dad,' Mum says. 'And . . . tell him I love him, would you?'

'I think he knows,' I say. 'But I'll tell him anyway.'

Somewhere in the graveyard, Zem barks. Presumably at a squirrel. Or maybe even a ghost.

'Zem?' says Mum, glancing in the direction of the fading sound.

I nod.

'Is he still burying your socks in the garden?'

'Whenever he can get them,' I say.

Mum smiles. 'That'll teach you not to leave them lying around on the floor.'

'I can't believe I'm being nagged about my laundry by a ghost.'

Mum laughs and the sound of it is like music.

She takes my hand in hers, turns it over and looks at the watch on my wrist. She smiles. 'It used to be mine,' she says. 'When I was little. That's why I gave it to you on your birthday. I understand why you were disappointed. I really do. And I'm sorry.'

'No,' I say, and my eyes are full of tears. 'I love it. I really love it.'

I remember my future self saying that this Mickey Mouse watch might have something to do with how I travel. He said it was about staying young. But thinking about it now, I think he was trying to say (or at least hinting in a very very roundabout way) that the reason I time travel is because – kind of like this watch – it's something I inherited from Mum. Which still doesn't explain how it happens. But maybe it explains why.

'Before I go,' Mum says, 'there's something I've been wanting to ask you from the second I got here.'

'What?'

'Can I have a hug?'

And if I was crying before, I'm sobbing my eyes out now. It's a good job there's no one else here to see – I'd never hear the end of it.

'Of course,' I say. And Mum wraps her arms around me and kisses me on the forehead. I close my eyes as she hugs me, and she feels warm and soft and real.

'I love you,' Mum whispers into my ear.

But while I hear her words, I feel no breath.

I open my eyes and Mum has gone.

'I love you, too,' I say.

Autumn is a long way off, but as I sit in silence, a single sycamore seed twirls and loops slowly downwards, coming to rest on the soil at the base of Mum's headstone. The church clock strikes the hour and the sound of the old bell is crisp and clear. I sit until the sound thins and fades to nothing. Like a ripple on the surface of a pond.

Then I stand up from the bench and call Zem.

It's sausages for tea tonight. I can't wait to see what Dad does with them.

NOT THE END

ACKNOWLEDGEMENTS

It takes a lot of people to bring a book into the world and I'd like to thank some of them here.

First, my agent, Stan, who's been in on this caper since I emailed him with the bare bones of an idea. This was his response: 'I think the idea is really exciting . . . but I'm completely lost by the cheese sandwich business.'

I immediately dropped the cheese sandwich (as it were) and the book is undoubtedly better for it. This is why we have agents. I'm grateful to have a very smart and exceptionally supportive one in Stan. As ever, sir, thank you.

And then there is Ruth Bennett, my editor. Here is what she said after reading it: 'I felt like I travelled back in time to being a kid as I read it. I am jumping with excitement at the prospect of bringing Andy – and

Bob! – to young readers.' Editors buy books from authors, and then make them (the books) better. Without Ruth's enthusiasm, insight and guidance, this book would be less funny and less exciting and unpublished. Bob and I thank you to the very end of time.

Other people without whom this book would either not exist, contain mistakes or look rubbish: Talya Baker, Jane Burnard, Nick Stearn, Emily Bornoff, Molly Holt, Isobel Taylor and Robin Boyden (those zombies!!). Everyone I have worked with on this book has been both smart and lovely – and I am very very thankful to you all.

And finally, Sarah, Ruby and Evie – thank you for your unwavering belief, patience and love xxx

ABOUT THE AUTHOR

Andy Jones began his career as an author writing novels for adults. Grown-up stuff about falling in love, falling out of love, falling in love again and having babies. All of which he has experienced in his own life. More recently, he has been writing books for children. Crazy stuff about genies, monsters, time travel and zombies. None of which he has experienced in his own life. Andy is also the author of *Unleash Your Creative Monster: A children's guide to writing*, and the novel *Wishes Come in Threes*. Andy lives on the outskirts of London (the best part in his opinion) with his wife, daughters and an assortment of other creatures.

ABOUT THE ILLUSTRATOR

Robin Boyden lives in Cheltenham with his partner and their ridiculous fluff ball dog Lupin. Robin has worked in the industry for over a decade, creating illustrations for the likes of *The Guardian*, *The Times*, *The Independent*, Bloomsbury, Nosy Crow and Penguin Random House. He is also the author and illustrator of the graphic novel *Georgia and the Edge of the World* (David Fickling Books) and the picture book *Gerald Needs a Friend* (Frances Lincoln Children's Books). When Robin isn't at his desk drawing, he's usually regretting spending so much time at the desk because his back hurts. Otherwise, he's out in the garden talking to plants and misidentifying birds. His favourite colour is all of them.

Thank you for choosing a Piccadilly Press book.

If you would like to know more about our authors, our books or if you'd just like to know what we're up to, you can find us online.

www.piccadillypress.co.uk

And you can also find us on: